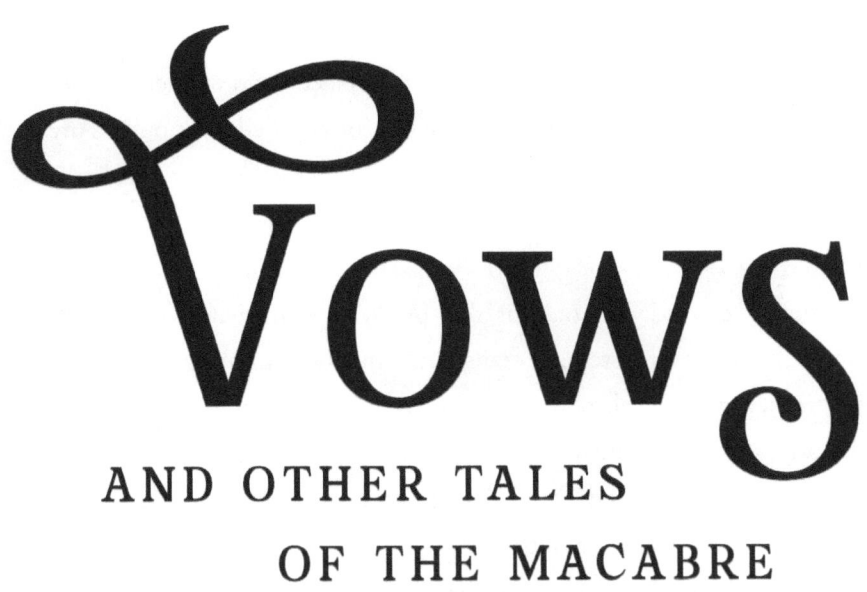

VOWS

AND OTHER TALES
OF THE MACABRE

ARJAY LEWIS

MIND
BENDER
PRESS

Published by:

Mindbender Press

474 South Main Street

Phillipsburg NJ 08865

www.mindbenderpress.com

Dedication

To lovers of good horror,
old and new.
You are my people!

Vows

Vows is a ghoulish little horror story I wrote years ago. *Sherlock Holmes Mystery Magazine* published it and featured my name on the cover. It's about devotion—the devotion that survives death itself....

Vows

··

It was a long drive from the city, as the rain dotted the windshield, and twilight descended. The young man I barely knew riding beside me in the passenger seat made the ride even longer.

"Penny for your thoughts." He smirked coyly.

"The night that lays ahead." I tried to sound enthusiastic.

"Me, too!" he said, and smiled.

With a desire to wipe the smile off his face, I grinned in a way I hoped looked sincere and thought of Vaneese.

I had to stay focused. After all, I needed this young cock-sure clown.

Anything for Vaneese.

How many men and women had it been? Since our wedding—

Do you, Frank, take this woman, Vaneese...

On a spectacular autumn day, with a clear-blue sky and golden leaves falling on the green grass, she and I were married.

She was a vision, dressed beautifully in white, red hair flowing around her stunning mix of French and Irish features.

She was the daughter of an aristocrat—what they once called a jet-setter. I was a successful software developer with money to follow her as she traveled the globe. I showed up at the same parties and casually ran into her. With time, charm, and persistence, I finally ended up escorting her. It took a year of pursuit until that glorious night where I presented her with a ring, and she said "yes."

—*to love, honor, and cherish...*

We spent a lengthy honeymoon on sun-drenched islands with beaches of pure white sand. We swam, ate, and made love as if it was our invention, never tiring of each other.

Until the headaches began.

The original diagnosis was in Bermuda. The local doctor insisted we fly to a hospital in South Carolina.

That's when they found the tumor.

An ugly knot of dark cells in her brain the size of a gumball.

And growing.

—*in sickness or in health...*

We moved to New York, close to what the doctors considered the finest cancer hospital in the world. Despite her diagnosis, or because of it, she became a dynamo, ready to fight the "annoying blob in my head," as she called it.

I was frightened but put on a brave face, day after day.

I would often sit up all night to watch her sleep, just to have a few more moments gazing at her.

The treatments made her fiery hair fall out, and she became rail thin with dark rings around her eyes, but she still carried that unique beauty.

The doctors tried combinations of chemicals, radiation, and treatments too vile to discuss. Soon, they told me there was no improvement, prescribing drugs that would ease the pain.

There was no more they could do.

Still, she went on. I don't know where she found the strength. Acupuncture, nutritionists, herbalists—she went to them all. Each day, her eyes grew more hollow and her hair did not return.

—*for richer, for poorer…*

The doctors gave her only weeks to live. Then one day, she met me at the door and told me of someone who could cure her.

The desperate look in her eyes worried me.

The woman arrived at eight, wrinkled as an apple doll, hair sprouting above her lip and from her ears. She wore a cheap floral dress on her heavy, sexless form and spoke with an accent from everywhere and nowhere.

"There are ways, ancient ways. You will go on… but not be… completely alive," she said, with the authority of an expert.

"Will I look like this?" Vaneese said, her hand going to her bald head.

"You will be beautiful again," the old woman said with a nod. "But it must be soon. The longer you wait, the more often you will need… to feed."

"Feed?" I asked. She ignored my question.

Instead, this appalling woman talked about money, naming an outrageous sum.

"That's a lot," I said, trying to hide my shock.

She glanced at Vaneese. "You must start tonight."

I put her off, telling her we would call the next day.

Once she left, I told Vaneese it was a scam, that this hideous woman was one of those evil people who preyed on the unwell.

Vaneese wouldn't hear of it. It was the only argument we'd ever had. Finally, too exhausted to quarrel, we went to bed.

She died during the night.

—forsaking all others…

When I woke next to her corpse, my first call should have been to someone else, anyone else. But no, I dialed the number the old woman left and begged for her help, incoherent with grief.

She told me to keep the room cool until she arrived. And to get money. It was now more, a lot more—a sum that would nearly wipe me out.

I was to tell no one.

In a daze, I went to the bank and spent two hours converting stocks, bonds, and accounts into cash, which I carried out in a briefcase. Was this wizened hag merely a thief? It didn't matter. Without Vaneese, what use did I have for money?

Arriving as the sun sank, she brought two dirty boxes of equipment and two muscular men as ugly as herself. She went into the bedroom and drew pentagrams and arcane symbols on the floor and walls.

She started a pot bubbling on a hot plate and chanted in a language I could not identify. I waited with the men. After several hours, as midnight approached, she ladled a dark mixture from the simmering pot into a cracked porcelain mug.

"Do you love your wife, Mr. Jameson?" she said.

"Yes," I told her, my throat tight. "More than life."

She nodded her wizened head. "Then you will have to help her. She will need to feed often."

"Feed?"

"She will know what to do. But first!" she said with a gesture.

The two men held me with an iron grip and pulled my right hand forward.

"What are you doing?" I asked, as the hag pulled out a large knife.

"Shhh," she whispered, as if to quiet a child.

She slid the knife across my open palm, drawing blood. Still in the embrace of the men, she led me to the bed. She poured the smelly brew into Vaneese's mouth, still chanting, and followed the mixture with a drop of my blood from the blade.

"Eat, my dear," she cooed.

Vaneese's body twitched, as if coming awake. The woman held my hand to Vaneese's mouth, and she suckled the open wound as the woman chanted.

No longer needing to hold me, the men let me go.

Transfixed, I could not pull away. I laid down next to her and fell asleep as she drew blood from my hand.

How many hours we were there? I don't know? An entire day because when we woke, it was dark again. They'd cleaned the house of the arcane symbols, and the case with the money was gone. The cut on my hand had closed as well.

Vaneese yawned, stretched, and rose from the bed, looking the picture of health. Her beauty had returned. She looked like her old self, my dear sweet Vaneese. Even her hair had grown back long, full and ablaze with color.

But she was different. There was something behind her eyes—a fierceness.

The first change was she slept during the day and could only go out at night. I did as well, grateful just to be with her.

She also ate little.

A few weeks later, she deteriorated, her eyes growing sunken and her new hair turning ashen.

"What can I do?" I asked. "More blood?"

She shook her head. "I know what I need. I feel it, inside," she said, touching her chest. "Bring me someone."

"Someone?"

"A sacrifice," she said, her eyes boring into me, and for a moment they looked as red as her hair. "It doesn't matter who."

My head was spinning, but that night I wandered the streets of New York, trying to think of where I could find someone to bring to her. How could I do it? Trying to seduce a woman into coming home with me would feel like I was cheating on Vaneese.

I had walked to Greenwich Village. Then the idea struck me. I could find someone and not break my vows.

In only a block or two, I found a bar named The Fatted Calf, a known gay bar. The name attracted me, and I walked in, sat at the bar, and watched the crowd. It was easy to spot men on the prowl.

A burly fellow with a shaved head, large mustache, and a penchant for wearing black sat next to me. I felt reticent, but I bought him a drink. We talked, and I suggested I was just 'coming out', recently, admitting I was gay. I paid for dinner and drinks, and with some mild cajoling, I persuaded him to come home with me.

We took a cab to my apartment, and I brought him up. The high ceilings and fashionable address impressed him. I poured him a drink and slipped away to Vaneese, who hid in the unlit bedroom.

"I have him," I whispered.

She lay hidden in a dark corner of the room, but from what I could glimpse of her, she'd undergone a change.

A frightening one.

She was crouched like some kind of lithe cat, her eyes glowing a dark amber.

The smell of the grave was all around her.

"Yessss. Send him to me!" she hissed, gesticulating with a finger that was now a claw.

I invited the man into the dark bedroom.

"I like it with the light on," he protested as he stepped through the door.

Vaneese leapt on top of him. He gave one yell of surprise, which became a gurgle, as she ripped his throat out with her teeth.

I ran from the room in revulsion, shut the bedroom door, and with shaking hands, poured myself a drink as I listened to Vaneese's growls and the sound of ripping flesh.

She fed.

Finally, I fell asleep in a living room chair, only to be awakened with a start by Vaneese touching my cheek. She was beautiful again, and she'd washed while I slept. She kissed me and took my hand, leading me into the guest bedroom, where she threw me onto the bed and made love to me with a passion I'd only ever dreamed of.

As she rolled off me and relaxed into sleep, she said, "Oh, please clean up, would you?"

I lay with her and watched her, radiant, as she slept.

I forced myself to dispose of what remained. Fortunately, there was little left—blood-red bones with chunks of sinew attached that fit easily into a garbage bag. The bedroom was a good choice; the wood floors cleaned up easily.

Over the months, we found new techniques, finding the necessary 'participants' in unusual ways. We found people who were interested in being with a couple. Vaneese would convince a man or woman to come home with the pair of us, stating that her husband "liked to watch."

Vaneese looked sickly again today, but after tonight, she will again have weeks of good health. Prepared, I had rebuilt my fortune, and regularly visited several "hot spots," and was quick to buy drinks and be friendly. It's amazing how easy it is when you are friendly and willing to spend a little money on someone.

This current young man was another empty-headed fellow looking for a 'Sugar Daddy.'

However, the news lately showed reports about men and women who frequented sex clubs were disappearing in the city.

This time, I made it a point to offer my 'friend' a weekend at my home in the mountains.

I was still driving, and he had moved his hand onto my lap.

I hadn't had to actually have sex with one of these 'choices'. I still hadn't broken my vows.

"Gonna be quite a night," he said, stroking me.

"Yes," I said hoarsely, behaving as though I were overcome with lust.

When we get to the cabin, it will be Vaneese he meets. And then…his maker.

Anything for Vaneese.

—*Until death do you part.*

Siren

For those of you who prefer science-fiction for your scares instead of gothic, here's a quick look at how a person might serve a prison term for their crimes in the future. I write stories that scare me. Imagine what it would be like having Siri or Alexa directly connected to your brain. I can't think of anything worse...or more frightening.

Siren

●●

*A*djusting *vertical stabilizer…*
CHIP's voice droned in the back of my head, inside my mind, forcing me to respond. My response was automatic.

Vertical stabilizer reset with course correction.

Forward scanners set to maximum…

Full scanning sweep. Can it still hear me?

Do not understand. Please restate the query.

They programmed CHIP to understand me. Nothing but logic. Nothing but precise direction would compute in its brain… in my brain.

Query discontinued. It's so deep inside my head with me. I can still shut myself off, but it's difficult.

Registering data from forward scanners.

Analyze all data, and inform of any results. There! That should keep the machine busy for a few minutes.

So I can think...

That's what I need to do. Try to remember that I'm a goddamn human being. Damned, that really is the best analogy. I'm damned with this thing connected to my *brain—*

Analysis complete. Not registering usable materials.

Continue scans.

Scans complete. Analysis complete. Not registering usable materials.

The machine is too smart for its own good. No, too smart for mine.

Do not understand. Please restate instructions.

Can it read me, even when I don't want it to? It didn't in the past, but that was long ago.

Years...

Do not understand. Please restate instructions.

Adjust the horizontal stabilizers by forty-five degrees and begin new scans.

Understood.

That should take a minute or two. I have to make sure it has things to do, so it doesn't set off the siren. As a kid, I always hated loud alarms, held my ears, and thought nothing could be worse.

Then, they hooked me up to this machine where the alarm goes directly into my brain.

I passed out the first time.

Now I can tolerate the noise, and it only uses the siren when it has to keep me under control.

It's much too easy to float on a cloud of its instructions.

I had a life once.

I think of Nicki and that summer by the shore. We made love under the dock, on that deserted beach. She clung to me, her fingernails clawed the skin of my back—

Adjustment complete. Beginning scans.

The feel of her under me, the scent of the sea, the sand wet against my knees, the—

Increased levels of respiration. Are you in distress?

NO! Dammit, I can't even fantasize without this machine—

Scans complete. Data inconclusive.

Reset scanners with modulating frequencies and re-initiate.

Understood.

What good is it to get mad? It's doing what it's supposed to do, the soulless, mindless collection of processors. Then again, CHIP 6000 is my only companion—

CHIP. Do you need me?

NO. Continue scans.

It reads my thoughts on a deeper level. Over time, it upgraded the interface between us. Perhaps in another six months or a year, there won't be a "me" at all. I won't be human, just an interface—

Scans complete. Potential material in Section 28.95.

Adjust course to those coordinates. Set the speed for most efficient fuel use.

Understood. Fuel levels are at—

I am aware of the fuel level. Please adjust the thrusters to maximize fuel efficiency.

Understood.

How long ago did they connect this damn machine to me? I'm not sure. Time passes both slowly and quickly here. I could be an old man by now.

I was thirty when they launched me into space. What year was that? It was right after the Harvest Festival. I know because I saw Nicki the last time before my sentencing.

CHIP!

CHIP. Do you need me?

What year is it? No, no—query restated. What is the date?

Digital calendar oh-three-point-oh-five-point-forty-two. I can restate in the Julian calendar, Lunar calendar—

Unnecessary. Continue primary instructions.

Understood.

Five years, is that all? Five years of the worst solitary confinement ever devised by man. I would have preferred the Spanish Inquisition with red-hot pokers or a Southeast Asia prison camp with bamboo under my fingernails.

At least I'd see other humans, if only when they'd torture me.

Instead, I'm in a sterile, self-cleaning environment hooked directly to a machine. The machine recycles my wastes. I'm automatically fed and watered like a hothouse plant. It sounds so much better than the dirty prisons of old. But at least there I could see the face of my tormentor. I could be alone with my own thoughts.

At least there I could hope.

Increased levels of respiration and cardiac activity. Are you in distress?

Yes, I am in distress.

What is the nature of the distress?

I want to get out of here!

Do not understand. Please restate instructions.

Disregard statement. I am not in distress. Continue primary instructions.

Understood.

It watches me without rest. And if I do anything it doesn't like, that siren blasts in my head. It limits my sleep to the hours it gives me, and it's never enough. I guess that's all part of the plan. Make me fall into a waking dream—

Five years.

I'm sure it sounded like a good idea to the bureaucrats, a use for the outcasts of society.

It started when the power grid switched to Galvanesium, that remarkable high-energy element which could supply the electrical needs of a continent.

Unfortunately, the stuff isn't indigenous to Earth: it's only found on asteroids. Plus, the converters burn the stuff up every few years.

Galvanesium miners became the richest men in history. It was the only way to get anyone to go into space to search for the stuff. A lot of them died when they tried—hoping to cash in on one rich find.

Legends grew because they found empty ships in this part of space—the crew gone.

That's still a mystery.

With these guys getting paid so much, the government pushed for mining ships that could operate with artificial intelligence. What did those prototypes do? Screwed up. Seemed like AI wasn't smart enough to comprehend self-survival, or if it did, it would go too far and destroy other ships to protect the mined ore in its hold.

Leave it to scientists and the government to come up with a solution. CHIP: the Cerebral Human Interface Protocol. An artificial intelligence interfaced with a human mind. Trouble was, who were you going to get to go into space hooked up to a machine?

There's always a solution.

Instead of the death penalty, they condemn convicts to spend their lives inside these machines. A spacecraft that uses a limited amount of resources, requiring periodic returns to base, so no space jockey could fly off into deep space. If he tried, good old CHIP would turn the ship around and bring him back.

They also let you know what happens if you try to break free, pull out wires, and force a return to base. On the first offense, they amputate your hands. Second offense, they cut off your legs.

After that, they get more personal.

After all, you don't really need limbs to work the ship.

I'm hooked up to the main viewing panels, and I can observe open space and watch instrument readouts. Hell, they even let me play an occasional game of solitaire.

I don't really "see" any screens—my eyes are closed. It goes directly into my brain, giving me a panoramic view.

It's still a prison.

Surgery implanted the interface. Then they hooked up the padded collar and restraints on both wrists to measure my pulse and keep my hands in a safe position. Then they lowered me into that padded metal pod.

It resembled an ancient Iron Maiden more than anything else. Something that needed limited oxygen and atmosphere. It can be easily and efficiently cleaned, while my body atrophies from lack of use.

But the machine keeps my mind busy.

Who'd have thought I would end up here? I was an honest guy. If not for Nicki, with a body that would make any man sell his soul to the devil.

Or commit murder.

I've had plenty of time to go over the details. What if she wasn't married? What if he hadn't been so involved with the space mining program?

How about what if he wasn't an abusive son of a bitch?

I saw the scars he'd left on her. In fact, I went over every inch of Nicki's body and examined every centimeter.

But he beat her, threatened to kill her if she left. I met with him to talk. We'd been friends once. He tried to choke the life out of me, and I smacked him on the side of the head with the first thing I could grab: a large metal award he'd won for his space work.

It killed him instantly.

Nicki panicked, and we tried to hide the body, and when they found it after all our denials, it appeared premeditated.

Forget that. It's all pointless.

I want to remember only Nicki, our last meeting. It's the one thing the machine can't take from me. I was free on bail, and we spent that day making love for what would be the last time. The scent of her skin, the feel of her.

She promised that if they found me guilty, she would come for me. Even out in space.

Impossible. They made me a part of this machine: a cog, another relay in the unending search for a power source. There's no rescue; there's nothing anyone can do. I'll go back to base, either with ore or empty. They'll give me a physical and send me back out again. With that voice in my head as my only company.

The noise shrieked in my head with such volume that I cried out. The sound of my scream unheard in the alarm's howl.

Shut it off, shut it off. You have my attention.

Alert! Unknown vessel approaching.

Display vessel, scan, and give complete information.

Understood. The vehicle is of an unknown design.

A picture appeared as it approached. It was an odd-looking thing: cylindrical, a flat surface in the front with a large back, I guess for engines. The surface wasn't smooth, but bumpy.

CHIP babbled the statistics, weight, and whatever else.

Life signs, I interrupted.

One.

Species?

Data inconclusive. Scans cannot penetrate the vessel efficiently.

Best guess?

Please restate the query.

Give a logical assumption based on the currently available data.

Human.

The idea settled in my mind for a moment. I was stunned. It was lovely to have a genuine emotion after so long experiencing only CHIP or memories.

Did you say human?

Data inconclusive. Scans cannot penetrate the vessel effectively.

I understand.

This ship bore no markings and was impossible to scan. Clever. Who could make such a vessel?

My heart skipped a beat. Nicki's dead husband had been filthy rich.

They did not consider Nicki an accessory in the crime. She had remained free.

Had she built this shadow vessel? Her deceased husband's company built spacecraft. He built the one I was in. Some called it poetic justice that I ended up hooked up to something created by him and built by his company.

Increased levels of respiration and cardiac activity. Are you in distress?

I am nervous because of the unknown vessel. Can you open a frequency for communication?

Will attempt standard greetings.

Forward responses to me.

Overridden. CHIP must follow standard contact procedures.

The machine will attempt communication. But only to repeat built-in warnings that this is an automated vessel that contains a dangerous criminal. Then it will start evasive maneuvers.

If it were Nicki, could I stop it?

Any luck?

Do not understand. Please restate the query.

Are we receiving communications?

No response to standard greetings.

Keep trying.

Understood.

That's when I heard it. A distant crackle, a distortion in the voice. But she'd have to use an unconventional channel so that it wouldn't register to the machine.

Paul?

The communications crackled and sputtered, but I could hear it clearly enough. Like music coming from a million miles away.

Nicki?

Increased levels of respiration and cardiac activity. Are you in distress?

Nicki, can you hear me?

Paul? Oh, God, I hear you.

Her voice, so much like music, filled my mind—

Increased levels of respiration and cardiac activity. Are you in distress?

Yes, I was in distress. I could feel my heart race inside me. I clenched and unclenched my hands, though they seemed like they belonged on someone else's body.

Five damn years, and I'd given up hope so long ago—

I needed a plan.

The alarm screeched through my brain again. That damned siren—

Increased levels of respiration and cardiac activity. Preparing emergency sedative.

CHIP. I am not in distress. Disengage sedative.

The noise stopped, and I tried to clear my head, which ached from the two recent alerts. I had to do something—

Prepare to dock with the vessel.

Override. Cannot establish docking with an unauthorized vehicle.

Vessel is Earthnorm. It is bringing fuel.

Cannot establish docking with an unauthorized vehicle. The vehicle has not communicated on the established frequency.

I will establish communication. Will you institute docking if I confirm communications?

There was a moment of silence, very rare, since CHIP usually processed things in a lot less time than I could.

The machine appeared puzzled. It had to consider all the possibilities of my orders. And I'm sure there were billions of them.

Understood. This meets criteria. I will allow you to interface with communications for five minutes.

Backups on backups.

Nicki?

Paul, I'm here.

Her sweet voice, like water, poured over me. I thought of all the stolen hours we shared away from the world and private things only we could know. Could CHIP know my deepest secrets?

Nicki, do you remember the shore?

Yes, Paul. I remember being under the dock most of all.

We were on the same wavelength.

We need to communicate in that same way.

There was silence, except for the crackle of static.

I understand.

Alert! Unauthorized vessel shifting to collision course.

That's right, you bastard.

Do not understand. Please restate instructions.

We're about to dock, sucker.

Override. Cannot establish docking with an unauthorized vehicle. Initiating evasive maneuvers.

CHIP, fast as he was, wasn't as fast as Nicki's ship. I heard the loud clunk even through the bulkhead, and my ship shook with such force, my body smacked against the padded walls of my prison.

The siren went off again. My mind stung from the incessant howl, the cry of the wounded beast that was my ship.

Alert. Major systems damaged. Main power is offline—

Nicki! You did it!

Paul, I'm waiting for you. I want to hold you.

The image of her naked under me—

—main ore storage facility, communications—

Yes, I want you, Nicki.

That damn siren. I had to shut it off.

CHIP. Disengage alarm.

The siren stopped.

CHIP. Emergency power only.

Emergency escape protocol.

There was silence. CHIP was not having a good day.

Emergency escape will disengage the interface.

Check your programming, CHIP. If the ship becomes damaged, you are to jettison me with a beacon.

Communications are not operational.

I could die, CHIP. You're programmed to keep me alive.

The siren blared through my head again.

Shut that damn thing off!

Alert! An unauthorized vehicle is attempting to dock.

Jettison me, CHIP.

There was silence, as if he wanted to activate the alarm, but knew it was pointless.

Alert! The unauthorized vehicle is not Earthnorm--

I felt an odd silence as the interface disconnected. Blackness and a deep hiss. I was suddenly aware of my body, locked in a padded coffin.

I lay naked in this shell, bindings attached to my hands, my feet, even a tube to my penis. But they were coming loose.

I was suddenly choking. The feeding tube in my throat. I squirmed my right hand free and pulled it out. I wanted to vomit, but I swallowed and fought the urge, surprised at the loudness of my breath and the choking noises I fought to control.

The only illumination was a small communications board. I looked up at the flickering red lights with my own real eyes.

A small glass panel read, "Communications offline".

I hit the override button. I knew what she was doing. Nicki, clever girl, blocked outside communications.

Nicki—

Could I still contact her without the interface?

Paul?

She heard me. And her voice, with all of its specific intonations, made me think of spring, of perfume—

Can you pick up my capsule?

Yes, darling. I can't wait to be with you.

A pang of fear went through me. Running my fingers over my face, I felt the beard. I examined my chest; the ribs were sticking out. I was suddenly afraid that after all this effort, she would take one look and I would disgust her.

Nicki, I've changed. Five years—

I love you, Paul. Come to me.

I sighed. Her voice was so beautiful. I wanted to laugh and cry.

I felt my pod shake, and there was movement. Artificial gravity under me. My limbs felt heavy for the first time in years.

Paul, how do I get you out?

The red switch—the emergency release.

My prison opened with a hiss as the seal broke. A pinkish-red light poured into my capsule as the small square opened above me.

I reached behind my head and disconnected the cable stuck to the plug in my skull. I pulled myself up, my hands all pins and needles, as they were called on to move for the first time in so long. I grunted and slipped through the opening. A man born from a mechanical womb.

I fell to the floor. It was odd material. Wet and warm. The light was subdued, but it blinded me. I fought to sit up, blinking.

I felt limbs go around me, pull me upright, touching me in a hundred places.

"Paul," Nicki's voice said, even sweeter.

"Nicki," I murmured as I tried to touch her.

She pulled the foam cushion from around my neck. The crunch of the Velcro was deafening. From the sensory deprivation of my capsule, everything seemed so loud.

She moved me to what I guessed was a bed, warm and soft, yet squishy under me.

"Paul, darling. You're safe," Nicki's voice sang.

I couldn't see yet; the light was too bright, but I could make out a shape and hear her sweet voice.

Something like a tentacle connected to the interface plug on the back of my skull.

The interface connected.

I knew.

This wasn't Nicki's ship.

This wasn't a ship at all. It was the lifeform CHIP detected.

It was alive.

And hungry.

I understood in my heart what had happened to the empty ships found in this region. The crew were called by this living vessel, which sang to their brains with memories of loved ones.

It brought me to it. Now, it would consume the life in me.

I was as trapped here as I had been in the machine.

Then reality faded. I was with Nicki, my beautiful Nicki. We would make love until I was exhausted. Then we would sleep and hold each other.

I enfolded a shape—Nicki—my memory of her in my arms

The Dark

This was my first attempt at a horror tale, eventually bought and published in the *H.P. Lovecraft Magazine of Horror*.

However, the writing of it inspired two important books for me. First, when I started writing this tale in June 1999, a truck hit Stephen King in Maine. The event and the odd notion that the story itself wanted to be written, inspired me to come up with the concept for my novel, *The Muse.*

Second, I turned this simple story into a full-length novel called *Kept In The Dark*, which differs from the short story. It has layers of history combined with a very different origin for Jake Hurd and the other characters.

The finale of *Kept In The Dark* is much bigger, as Jake ended up being a much more heroic character than I originally envisioned him.

As a side note, my first job after high school was as a night guard.

The Dark

....

J ake Hurd never got used to the dark. It wasn't the darkness itself as much as the things that were hiding in it.

That's why I became involved. I'm a licensed psychiatrist in the great State of New Jersey. I deal with the crazies, the misfits, the insecure and, of course, the people who see things.

When I was called in on the case, I thought it was no big deal. Human beings are afraid of the dark; it's a common primeval fear that strikes us as children. As adults, we try not to let it overpower us, at least until we find ourselves some place gloomy and unsafe, at which point most of us become the frightened prey of our prehistoric past.

Dr. Bill Benning is an old friend and a good golf partner. When he called me in on the case, he told me I would have to keep it very hush-hush. The patient was a security guard and considered some kind of poster boy for guards.

Now that's an image!

The security company wanted us to keep his head screwed on until he reached retirement in another five years.

Agreeing to a fee larger than my usual, I felt I could give this case top priority with low publicity. It would be easy. A man who spends his time walking through dim hallways alone has ample time to dream up nightmares. I decided with some time on the couch, a few visualization exercises and an antidepressant or two, he would be fine.

Then I met him.

Jake must have been tall when he was younger: 6'5" or 6'6". However, over the years, his shoulders slumped. I really didn't expect a man of fifty-nine years old to look closer to seventy-nine. Most of his hair was gone, leaving wisps of white at his temples and a flesh-colored dome on top.

They held him at the hospital for observation because of a suicide attempt.

He walked into my office wearing his hospital gown and a robe. Scars covered his legs, the result of numerous cuts and gouges. Whatever he was doing to himself, the slashing of his wrists wasn't the first time he'd cut himself.

I invited him to sit down. "So, Jake--can I call you Jake?"

"I don't mind," he said.

"I understand you've been having troubles, Jake."

"That's what they tell me," he answered.

"Do you want to talk about it?"

"That depends," he said, staring at me, as if watching my every reaction. "Do you really want to know? I mean, the entire story?"

"Whatever you want to tell me," I suggested.

An odd smile crossed his lips, and he said, "Okay, but you asked. It began forty years ago." And he told me the story of his life.

Jake hadn't planned to live his life in the night, walking obscure hallways and lightless stairwells. In fact, when he was a young man, the idea of being a security guard struck him as a joke, something to do for a year or two.

As a therapist, I thought this was a healthy attitude. A lot of security guards want to be cops and act like they are one.

Jake started his first assignment at nineteen. He applied to the security company after seeing an ad in a newspaper. It was a dirty, cluttered office, but they immediately offered him a position working midnight to eight AM. The company didn't train him; they just gave him a uniform and sent him to the job site. On his first night, another guard showed him the rounds.

The watch clock, a large, heavy circular machine with a clock face and an oversized keyhole, fascinated Jake. He would walk through the darkened factory, and at each checkpoint, he would locate a large metal key chained to the wall. He'd insert the key into the clock and move on. The key would make a mark on a paper strip inside the contrivance, noting the time and location.

That first night, as the other guard walked him through the gloomy factory, Jake looked at the areas that seemed to be in permanent shadow. He couldn't fight the odd feeling that there was something there. This instinct grew as he did the rounds by himself.

"Something?" I interrupted. "Can you be a little more specific?"

"Yes," Jake said, nodding. "It was like eyes were watching my every move. It was as though the dark was aware of me."

I wrote a note on the pad of paper in my lap and asked him to continue.

Jake said that he ignored the feeling, swallowed his fear, and did the rounds anyway. In fact, he did them deliberately slowly. He wanted to get a glimpse of whatever was hiding in the gloom. Shining his flashlight into corners, he hoped to catch a glimpse. He turned on the light switches when he detected movement, trying to catch whatever was there in a sudden flood of light.

Whatever lived in the lightless areas was too quick, too clever. Jake could never catch them, but he knew they were there.

"That's all we have time for today," I said. "I'll see you tomorrow."

Jake agreed, and an orderly took him back to his hospital room. I went about the rest of my day, but that night, I found I had trouble sleeping.

On my next session with Jake, I was tired and bleary-eyed, but I pressed on.

"What did you do at night on your rounds, when you felt these eyes watching you?" I asked.

"Thinking and planning; there was time for both."

Jake went on, telling me he stayed at that factory until it closed ten years later. By now, the security company had positions in offices in pleasant buildings, but they moved him to another factory, just as bleak and uninteresting. The company liked him;

he showed up on time, did his rounds with a diligence few others possessed. The company didn't know he was looking for things in the shadows.

"That was thirty years ago," Jake mused.

The new location, as dull and depressing as the previous one, was actually a relief at first. For days, he thought the eyes weren't there. Jake felt calmer, relieved, as if maybe the whole thing had been in his mind.

But, in less than a week, he sensed them again—sometimes just around a corner or watching him from above—wherever there were unlit places for them to hide.

However, there were some advantages.

He met a secretary whom he talked to every morning. Finally, he worked up the nerve and asked her out. Jake said she was about average height, with average looks and average needs, but she was a little dynamo of energy.

He found her positive and upbeat personality a refreshing change from the dreary thoughts that pervaded his own mind.

They married, and a daughter was born less than a year after the wedding.

"I guess back then I was as happy as I've ever been," Jake said, but the look on his face didn't suggest happiness.

The schedule of working nights meshed well with the requirements of his wife's daytime position. With a slight change in her arrival time and they could both raise their child. She was home in the evening and at night. He was there during the day and slept in the evening. The daughter flourished and grew, supervised and loved by one parent or the other.

"I wish we'd had more than one," Jake said. "But my wife wouldn't hear of it."

As furtive eyes watched Jake during the night, he found they didn't stay at the factory. They followed him during the day, at home, and in his darkened bedroom.

He would sleep and suddenly jump up and pull open the curtains with a yank to let the sunlight pour in, trying to catch the intruders.

His behavior frightened his wife and daughter.

"If they had just helped me!" Jake said.

"What would that have done?" I pointed out.

"Then maybe, just maybe, I would've caught them," Jake lamented.

That ended that session, and I wrote up my notes. This was going to be an interesting case, after all. I thought I could get a psychiatric paper out of Jake and his 'things in the dark'.

Unfortunately, I would have to report advanced paranoia, schizophrenia, and delusions to the security company.

That night I slept little. I left the light on in the bathroom, which was reassuring, but ultimately didn't help.

The next day, Jake told me he made elaborate traps to catch his shadowy adversaries, whatever they were. He would prove the creatures were real.

He tried to explain to his wife and little girl why these odd contrivances were important, and they needed to be careful around them.

His wife thought them a danger and was getting more and more upset by Jake's behavior.

"I just wanted to protect us," he said. "To scare those things off, to get them to bother someone else."

He bought lights that were powerful and bright to fill every inch of the house with safe, white light.

It was on one of those lamps that his little girl burned her hand

She accidentally tripped over a power cord, and the heavy light, balanced on a three-legged stand, fell over on her. They needed to go to the hospital, where the doctor said the broken and burned hand would never be the same.

The next day, his wife got a court order, and Jake couldn't go home anymore.

She also filed for divorce, for mental and emotional cruelty.

"That was twenty years ago," Jake fretted. "When the divorce became final."

Jake moved to a small apartment, the child support making it necessary to live simply. He didn't really mind. It was smaller, easier to light, easier to build traps. He became fixated on electronics.

He had limited visits with his daughter. Also, the court sided with his wife in ordering that he couldn't talk to the child about the creatures.

That he found difficult.

"I mean, how can she protect herself if she doesn't know what to look for?" Jake said, exasperated.

Ultimately, Jake accepted it, deciding it was for the best. After all, this way the things couldn't overhear him talking about a trap. That made it more possible for him to catch them unawares.

"You mean, the things might have overheard you talking about what measures you were taking?" I said, attempting to understand.

"Of course, Doc," Jake said, as if it were obvious.

That was how that session ended, with Jake looking at me as though I were dense.

That night, as I left a late-night group therapy session, I had the strangest sensation that I was being watched. I chortled to myself; Jake's stories were affecting my perception.

Even so, that night I slept in the guest room with the light on. With the light, I could finally sleep through the night.

In the next few sessions, Jake told me that a larger outfit, which still kept Jake's services, had bought the security company. They moved him often from location to location. He was walking a shift where a computer could track his rounds. Now he carried a key and inserted it into strategic wall-mounted keyholes.

He didn't tell any of the changing array of coworkers about his interests.

He showed the supervisors some of the motion detectors he'd designed. The company bought the rights to several of Jake's inventions, gave him awards, credit, and a hefty percentage of the profits for some of his innovations.

The equipment was cutting-edge, and it was helping the company grow and prosper.

I slowly understood why Dr. Benning had brought me in on the case in such a quiet way. The company didn't want the public to know that their innovator, the man behind some of their best security tools, was a raving paranoiac.

Jake invented machines to catch the things in the dark, and he hoped if his company used them, he would have the chance to use them on a larger scale. He found, however, that it was the same problem as when he changed locations. The devices would keep them away for a while, but eventually, they would figure it out and return.

In fact, once the things learned how a device worked, it wouldn't even hamper them. They still watched Jake from the shadows.

"Then about ten years ago, I heard them," Jake said.

"Hear them?" I repeated, as If I misunderstood.

"Well, I guess you'd say I noticed their sounds."

Jake told me it was small, quiet noises to begin with, rather like the wind passing through dry leaves. As Jake listened more intently, he heard the creature's murmuring just beyond his consciousness.

"Were they saying anything?" I asked.

"No," Jake said. "Just strange noises. Maybe they were talking to each other, but not to me. Their tones and frequencies seemed to be part of the background, but I learned how to listen for them."

Jake was still building his traps and alarms and selling them to the company. His daughter was in college, and the money helped. He was making enough to buy a house, but his apartment was his bunker.

Being aware of their sounds, Jake possessed a new weapon in his arsenal. He tried to follow the creatures not just with his sense that they were there, but with his ears.

As he continued to do his rounds, he would listen for them, so he could wait until they were close, turn on his flashlight, and hear them scurry away.

"I enjoyed that," Jake said with a smile. "I would even sit some place dark, wait for them to come and flip on the lights, so they had to flee."

"You were frightening them for a change," I said.

"I guess," said Jake, swallowing hard.

"Tell me, Jake, you were a success with your company. Why didn't you ask to be transferred to the day shift?"

Jake looked at me as if I were crazy.

"They offered me a day job. Offered to make me head of a whole damn department." His voice dropped conspiratorially. "But I couldn't. I had to sleep during the daytime. When it was safe."

This was Jake's life. Sleeping during the day, even on days he didn't work, then tinkering with devices in the early evening and working midnight to eight at a security post. He became a captain and did more paperwork, but he insisted on doing one round a night "to stay in shape".

"Wait a minute," I interjected. "Was that the real reason?"

"Of course not," Jake said. "But that's what I had to tell them."

Jake used that round to study the noises from the darkness. He wanted to keep his ear trained so he could reproduce the sounds.

"I guess during this time I became less afraid of them. That was a mistake. I also figured a way to catch some of them, really catch them, not like the other times." Jake looked at his feet. "I guess that was a mistake, too."

"Jake, how did you think you could catch one of these things?"

"I made a detector, and it was a beauty. A small sonic device that could be fine-tuned to almost any frequency, even as faint as the wind." Jake smiled at the memory. "I could attach it to anything; an alarm, a phone, or even a powerful halogen light."

Jake elaborated with excitement about these lights, which were very new. They created an astounding amount of illumination quickly. He persuaded the security company to let him run trials with the new lights.

He set up in a large open space in the factory. It was several hundred square feet, and he could fill it with a dazzling light. Even with tests done during the day, the light output required Jake to wear protective goggles.

"When it was finally ready, I made a little remote control to turn on the detector. Then that night I waited until three--maybe four in the morning. I went to that section of the factory and sat in a chair, stock still," Jake told me.

He used a large, dark part of the warehouse, a storage area filled with display pieces that the factory put up at Christmas time. Big boxes of artificial trees and mechanical elves lay strewn in unnatural positions.

He knew it was the creatures' favorite place.

He sat utterly still, waiting for their sounds. Their little clickety-clacks and whispers in the dark. In the distance, he could hear the water pumps and the air conditioning units as they gushed and chugged away.

Waiting in total darkness, he listened for their undertones.

There was a silent tap that he recognized. He held still, his finger on the button that would activate his sonic apparatus.

More taps came, his thumb at the ready, waiting for them to draw closer. Breathing as lightly as he could, he fought to not to make even the faintest sound.

Moving in the shadows, he felt them all around him, making their little noises, the ones he worked so hard to adjust his sonic equipment to register.

Would the detector hear those faint whispers, or was it all in his mind?

He pressed the button.

The lights shot on with a dazzling impact. Jake was wearing his special goggles   to protect his eyes from the blinding illumination.

"That's when I saw them," he said.

"You saw them?"

"Yes, in the light, with no place to run and no shadows to hide in. For a moment, I could see them."

I was stunned. This was entirely against standard paranoid behavior. I was afraid Jake might be severely delusional. I asked him, "What did these things look like?"

"Like shadows," Jake said. "Flat and two-dimensional beasts with square heads and jagged lines that were their eyes and mouths. They looked at me, angry, and then they were gone. They ran away to hide in the darkness, somewhere else."

After that session, I started looking through my Physician's Desk Reference. I hoped to find a drug that would help in a case where the patient appeared rational but was as far gone as Jake.

It would've been easier if I hadn't kept needing to adjust the lights. The shadows in my room seemed too close.

In further sessions, Jake told me he had tried to trap them again, this time with a special camera to record them. But the creatures didn't take the bait. They knew where he set up the lights and wouldn't return.

The days stretched into weeks.

"It was kind of nice," Jake said. "I actually slept a couple of nights and visited my grandchild one day. My daughter had a little girl around that time, and I finally had time to see her."

Jake hoped the creatures were gone. But he was wrong.

When they came back a few weeks later, it was different. They were no longer content to watch him.

They were angry.

"That was five years ago," Jake said. "They had become different, more aggressive."

At first, when Jake was aware they were back, he thought it would be the same as it had been before. But now, sometimes, he felt them touch him. At first it was fleeting, like a butterfly passing over his skin.

It almost scared Jake to death

Then it escalated. Small touches became harder, more often, to let Jake know who was in charge.

Then one night, Jake did his rounds on a post that required a walk through the machine shop. Jake no longer wore a uniform like a police officer. Instead, all the guards were in brown suits: more corporate, less cop.

He was carrying a device called a Morse gun, designed to fit into little plastic rectangles situated all over the factory. A computer chip in the gun timed and tracked his route. He had only five minutes to get to the next location.

As Jake walked into the machine shop, he knew they were there, invisible as they always were. But there were the noises, as if they weren't trying to hide at all. He walked by the different lathes, woodworking and metal cutting machines, silent in the night.

Something grabbed his leg!

Jake fell forward, smacking into a machine. He fell to the floor, his head bleeding profusely.

"That's how I got this," Jake said, pointing to the scar on his head. I assumed that Jake's old injuries were symptomatic of his mental state.

Self-mutilation is not uncommon in a delusional patient.

Jake grabbed his flashlight, getting back up on his feet. He shone the bright light wildly, trying to chase them away. He thought he saw one move through the beam, and Jake pursued it toward a large sheet metal cutter in the room's corner.

Jake kept catching glimpses of it, then he heard the big machine power up.

"They could actually turn on switches," Jake said excitedly. "I went to turn it off—that's when they tripped me."

"Tripped you?" I said.

"Pulled my legs clean out from under me," Jake said. He fell to the ground and tried to pull himself up.

"But something, one of them, was pulling on my hand."

Jake looked up to see his hand right under the huge cutting blade.

"I turned and rolled, pulling my hand free just as that blade came down," Jake said. Just remembering was making him sweat. "I got up unsteadily to my feet. But all around me, the machines started turning on." His eyes glazed over as the memory took him. "I ran out of the building, outside into the night air, but they kept tripping me. I had to use my radio to call for help."

His fellow officers found him outside the machine shop building, covered with mud and babbling incoherently. He went to the hospital and got five stitches in his head.

"How did you explain this to the other guards?" I asked.

"That was easy," Jake chuckled. "I told them I slipped in some oil, fell and hit my head. Hitting my head caused me to talk incoherently and fall in the mud."

"So, once again, you hid your obsession from others," I said.

"I didn't want them to think I was crazy," Jake explained. "After all, you think I'm crazy."

I sighed. This was a normal moment in therapy, but the one I always dreaded.

"Jake, you tried to take your own life."

Jake moved closer to me and spoke quietly and intently. "That's what they want you to think, Doctor. The last few years have been Hell. They kept doing things to me, not as big as the machine shop, but little things. Metal pieces moved into my path, knives, whatever they could get." He held up his wrists to show me the bandages. "They did this."

I quieted my tone to match his. "Okay, Jake. How did they do that?"

Jake sat back and inhaled deeply.

Jake told me he had grown tired of the endless pokes and bumps during the night. So, he planned to end it. He built another little device. A small strobe, no bigger than a camera flash, that could oscillate like a disco light, but much, much brighter. Jake had to outfit himself with a large battery pack, constructed like a vest under his clothes. The strobe itself was two small units he wore clipped on his belt under his jacket. All he would have to do was pull up his jacket and activate the strobes.

"And this time," Jake said. "I built a camera. A small one that I put in the belt buckle to take pictures while the strobes flashed. I figured then I'd have proof! Then people would have to believe me and help me get rid of them."

That night, wearing his special vest and belt, Jake took an early round around midnight and walked it. He could hear them, angry and grumbling in their whispering way.

Something touched his leg. He jumped, but he needed to get bolder.

"Come on, you cowards," Jake remembered saying. Moving to a part of the factory where there was open space, he led them into the cafeteria, which was big, open and had very few lights on.

He could hear them, feel them. They were grabbing at his legs and rubbing his bald head.

"This is it!" Jake yelled, pulling the jacket out of the way and activating the strobes.

It was the first time he had heard the things scream.

The lights blazed repeatedly, freezing the dark shapes in the flashing light. But it was dissimilar to the other time. The strobe light gave them depth, making them look three dimensional. They covered the slits of their eyes with their stunted limbs as they howled.

Jake roared as his little camera clicked away. "There you go, bastards!" he yelled.

This was it! He finally had his victory. That's when one of the little things grabbed a chair and shoved it against him. Then another hit him with a trash can. The others grabbed whatever they could and hit him, threw things at him.

"The connections to the strobes were far too delicate," Jake said. "They tore them loose and then they all pounced on me in the darkness."

As Jake told it, they threw him to the floor, smashed his lights, and then one of them came in with a huge knife from the kitchen.

Jake hit the button on his radio, yelling for help, but the creatures pulled his hands up, and the one with the knife neatly slit his wrists. As the blood poured down his arms, Jake blacked out, listening to the sound of his own screaming.

"I woke up here in the hospital. That's when you and I first spoke."

I put my pen down. "Jake..."

"It's all true," Jake said. "Read my medical report when I came in. There was bruising along my hips from the impact with heavy objects."

"Jake," I said. "You could have slit your own wrists and fallen against something. You're asking me to believe a lot with no proof."

Jake moved closer, whispering in my ear. "I've got the photos from my little camera."

"Jake, are you sure you didn't imagine this?"

"No, no," Jake whispered again. "But you should come to my room before nightfall. I'll give you the film. You can get it developed—then you'll have proof."

I said I would, and they took Jake back to his room.

I sat at my desk, going over my notes. This case was more than a psychiatric paper. Hell, Jake could be a book, even possibly a life's work.

I met with other patients, but for me it was a halfhearted effort, listening to them whine about their mothers. As soon as I had seen my patients for the day, I sat at my computer and transcribed my notes about Jake. I didn't really keep track of time until I looked up from my screen and saw it was ten o'clock.

I was supposed to meet Jake, but it was long after hours. It wasn't a good choice to leave someone who's afraid of the dark waiting at night. I saved my work and walked to Jake's room.

It was ghostly walking the hallways at night. The corridors always seemed so busy during the day. Now, the lights were dim, and I walked down hallways that were dark from end to end.

I turned. What did I hear? A sound, so quiet, yet so out of place. Of course, it was nothing. It had to be. I was letting Jake's stories and my imagination run wild.

I reached the main desk where the night nurse was on duty. Signing in, she told me the number of Jake's room. I walked down the hall, past the dim rooms, looking for Jake's.

It should be easy to find, since he asked that the light always be on. In fact, I put that request on his chart.

I looked for a doorway with a light on, but I didn't see one. Checking the room number, I realized I had walked right past it. I retraced my steps, reading the numbers as I went back.

I reached Jake's door, and it was ajar, but there was no light in the room. Some new orderly mustn't have read his chart and turned it off. I knocked on the door and pushed it a little more open.

"Jake?" I said.

No reply. They must have sedated him, and I'd have to wait for this film of his tomorrow.

I turned the light on, in case he woke up in the night and panicked.

Staring into the darkness, as I flipped the light switch, the fluorescent lights flashed and blinked. I saw something in the darkness for a moment.

It lasted only for the time the light flickered and strobed, but I saw it. About three feet high, a dark mass, like a shadow, with slits for eyes and a jagged line for a mouth.

It looked at me and hissed like a cat.

I yelled out. As the lights came on full, it was gone.

It had been standing near the bed, and now I could see Jake.

Sprawled on the bed, Jake's head was bent at an unnatural position, hanging off the side. Wrapped tightly around his neck was the bedsheet, so tight as to be choking. On his chest was a small thing, like a belt buckle, and a small roll of a thin film, laid out and exposed to the light, ripped and ruined.

My cry brought nurses and orderlies running. They ran past me and moved to Jake to see if they could save him. I couldn't move. The short dark thing's image embedded in my mind.

"So that's how Jake died?" Dr. Benning said. "These creatures from his mind killed him?"

"No, Doctor," I said. "Those things are real."

Dr. Benning rubbed his chin. Then he looked at his watch. "Look, Jake died falling out of his bed with a sheet wrapped around his neck. It was an accident."

I sighed and muttered, "It doesn't matter what you think. Protect me. They're after me, because I've seen one of them."

Dr. Benning shook his head. "I'm afraid that's all the time for this session. The orderly will take you back to your room. Please don't fight the nurses. Take your medication."

"Only if you give me the remote I asked for to turn on the lights in my room," I said.

"It's highly unusual, but I'll make sure they hook something up for you."

The orderly came in and escorted me back to my room. I could hear the nurses wander around mumbling under their breath about "the strain," and "poor fellow just went mad."

I don't care what they think.

In the night, with the light on, I sit and watch for them, always on my guard. I can hear them just beyond the bright safety of my light, scratching and tapping. I know they're waiting for me...

In the dark.

Dreamcatcher

Everyone needs their dreams, but what does one do when his or her dreams become nightmares? Perhaps take a walk in the woods? The dark woods where you are all alone? Or really not alone at all…

Dreamcatcher

....

I t all began with a fight.

One of those draining, cliché 'married couple' battles—heated arguments over money, chores, and who was pulling their weight in this sinking ship we called home. The same worn-out lines, old wounds flaring to the surface as if freshly opened. We'd long ago staked our claims, warily guarding our own territories, each unwilling to concede an inch.

Lately, things had been rough. A freelance writer for over a decade, my income was a mercurial beast—some weeks, steady paychecks rolled in; others, empty silence.

The strain of new car payments tipped us from survival into chaos. We weren't barely scraping by anymore—we were drowning just beneath the surface.

My wife... she's brilliant. Summa Cum Laude, a top-tier computer consultant with a steady job and ambitions I admired. But every morning, as she slipped out before dawn wearing a crisp blouse and determination, I sat in my bathrobe nursing coffee, and the tension grew thicker.

"I wouldn't mind," she snapped one morning, voice edged with exhaustion, "if you did something around the house."

I sighed, defensive. "Besides raising Joey, picking up after him, and getting dinner on the table—"

"Occasionally," she cut in, voice sharp.

"I—I load the dishwasher," I said, almost pleading.

"Yeah, and we both know how life-changing that is!" she shot back bitterly. "I'm the one making this house livable and bringing in the income, while Joey just started school. Could you maybe clean for a few hours? Or get a part-time job or something?"

I gritted my teeth. "Last month, that magazine paid me a grand—"

"After two months of nothing," she spat, her voice trembling with frustration. "The savings are nearly gone, and I'm watching us sink."

"So you want me to get a 'real' job? I thought we agreed—I'd write."

"If I saw any progress on your novel," she said, almost whispering now, bruised by disappointment.

"It's been weeks of writer's block. A novel isn't easy—"

"You've been writing that thing since before Joey was born," she said, voice cracking.

"So, a job?" I asked, voice low.

"Temporarily. Till we pay off the hospital bills—"

"That your damn insurance refused to cover," I growled.

"If you did a little more around here, just steady effort… then I could carry the load. Maybe you could write for the Book Review again—"

"Wow, yeah, reviewing others' work. Great idea," I snapped sarcastically.

"We all have to make sacrifices," her voice rose, raw and desperate.

Our words spiraled into a shouting match—bitter and loud, shredding the quiet of our late Saturday afternoon. Joey didn't seem to notice; absorbed in a cartoon world, a writer's son untouched by books.

When the shouting hit a crescendo, I slammed the door behind me and stormed out. Clad in my worn jogging suit, the one I threw on for aimless Saturdays, with sneakers and a light jacket, I grabbed my wallet—not that I planned to spend a cent —and got behind the wheel of the minivan she pays for.

I drove off into the setting sun.

The farm. Where else could I go?

I grew up just a few towns over, on a hundred acres of prime New Jersey farmland passed down through generations. My family never kept animals, but we grew crops—organically, before the world thought it was chic. Acres of hay were our cash crop, the heartbeat of our heritage.

Until I was eleven.

That's when the state swooped in and claimed it, converting the land into a wildlife protection area. My father called it a land grab—a forceful wrenching away of our legacy with little choice but to accept the market value offer. The farm's loss tore the soul from him, leaving a shadow where a man once stood strong. It's probably what killed him young.

It's no wonder I don't trust the government.

But the farm? Now it's public land. I can still go there. Since before marriage, my wife and I have driven every summer to picnic in that quiet sanctuary. I've always been at home on that soil.

Tonight, I needed to be there now.

I drove the ten minutes through Randolph and Ironia, the familiar towns blurring past my windows.

When I crested the hill just beyond the old General Store—now converted into a cozy pizzeria—I pulled into the small gravel lot.

The sun was sinking, painting the sky in brilliant shades of violet, bleeding beneath the towering trees like spilled ink. A calm that hardly matched the turmoil knotted inside me.

I left my wallet on the passenger seat, locked the door with a quiet click, and stepped onto the gravel. My sneakers stirred the stones with each step, crunching softly.

The cool spring air touched my face as I crossed the empty field. The winter's brown grass, brittle and dry, crackled underfoot along with last season's fallen leaves.

Ahead, the woods beckoned—my woods, at least in memory.

I grew up here, learning each landmark as a boy. Now, as an adult, everything seemed smaller, the plants thick and wild where once neat rows of crops had stretched.

Still, I recognized the ghost outlines: the place where the barn stood, the spot where the garage had been, even faint hints of the farmhouse foundation. The buildings had crumbled long ago, but the memories clung like shadows.

The woods themselves had always been my refuge. Rocky and unforgiving soil kept farmers from planting, and so trees flourished in an irregular band of pines, oaks, and especially birches—the slender white trunks standing in perfect ranks. They looked almost uniform; if you spin around in a grove of birches, you can't tell east from west.

Such eerie symmetry, and yet home.

Hundreds of times I had wandered these woods as a child. I remembered Indian Rock, famous for its cache of arrowheads, a silent testament to the tribes who came long before.

Scattered stones formed mysterious circles and crumbled foundations here and there—reminders of lives layered over centuries.

Usually, I walked the familiar path—starting near the vanished farmhouse, then deeper into the treeline. But tonight I deliberately reversed it, heading straight into the woods first.

Soon I stumbled upon one of those half-hidden stone circles, dark and polished smooth with age. The fading light, hushed by the coming night, gave the stones a sacred quality, as if they held secrets just out of reach.

I crouched in the center, tracing the cold surfaces with my fingers.

Suddenly, the argument with my wife flashed back. Words I'd spewed in frustration, echoes of blame and regret.

"If only," I whispered aloud, "If only I knew what to do... how to live..."

A thought startled me: *Or dying...?*

Why did that idea sneak into my mind uninvited?

I stood and shook off the chill creeping up my spine, suddenly aware of how foolish I must look talking to myself in the silence.

I left the circle, heading toward Indian Rock. These days it would have to be called Native American Rock, though I still knew it as Indian Rock. It was sacred ground, older than anything else here.

I felt odd, like changing my usual route had shifted something inside me. The sky was darkening faster than expected. I should have brought a flashlight from the car, but I was too eager to escape my thoughts, to feel the evening air on my face.

The early spring evening was pleasant—the world awakening after months of snow and ice. Daytime warmth lingered, though the cooling air made me wish for my gloves from my winter coat.

I climbed uphill, careful on loose stones and muddy patches left from recent rains, trying not to slip in the thickening dusk.

Then I heard it—a sharp, systematic tapping echoing among the trees.

Could it be someone? No, probably just an echo...

Then the thought of animals rose unbidden. Bears, I remembered from stories. Our old dog used to chase away bears near the house.

The tapping grew nearer. My steps slowed. Eyes strained against the gloom.

Suddenly, a flash of red feathers shot out from the brush—a startled woodpecker. It beat upward, flapping wildly as I stumbled backward with a startled yelp and landed hard on soft earth beneath the tree.

Looking up, I saw the bark stripped clean in neat rows—the woodpecker's handiwork. I laughed, my tension easing. Just a bird getting its last meal before dark.

I rose and continued, deciding this was the path I'd take. A few minutes past Indian Rock, then back to the van.

Simple and straightforward.

But my mind kept circling back to that argument—each cutting word replayed with perfect hindsight.

Did we really have to buy that house? Couldn't we have stayed in the cramped two-bedroom apartment, happy and free? But Joey was on the way, and her nesting instinct overpowered reason. So we bought big in White Meadow Lake.

Maybe I didn't help enough. I raised Joey mostly alone but let him binge on TV far too much so I could write. Or at least, that was the plan. The writing.

I used to churn out pages, ten a day, effortlessly. I envisioned the Great American Novel rising from me—a work that would be required reading decades from now. A bestseller that would let me quit chasing shallow freelance gigs and celebrity gossip.

The surrounding woods grew darker, broken twigs crackling beneath my boots. Then another sound—a rustle just beyond the reach of sight.

A squirrel? A groundhog? Maybe a raccoon. I recalled warnings about rabid raccoons—fleas, snarling teeth, infection sinking into flesh. The thought made me shiver despite the still-warm evening.

I told myself, "I'm fine. If I get bitten, I'll drive to the doctor. We have insurance. Medical insurance. Life insurance."

Two hundred and fifty thousand dollars. More than I'd earned in years.

Then, from my right, a rustling noise—close. Someone following me?

"Hello?" I called, voice rough.

Silence.

"Hello? Anyone there?"

My heart pounded so loud it drowned out everything but its own rhythm. I stood frozen in the thickening dark, panting, muscles tight.

Nothing moved.

"Talking to myself again," I muttered.

I turned to head back—the simplest circle back to the van.

But twilight descended fast, swallowing landmarks. I stumbled into unfamiliar patches, disoriented as if the birch trees themselves had shifted and now closed in around me like a maze.

Why had I changed my route? If I'd stuck to my usual path, I'd be near the—

There it was again—the sound. Quiet but deliberate footsteps crunching leaves a few feet away.

I stopped, breath catching. "Who's there?" I demanded, voice cracking.

No reply.

I considered the likely explanation—broken branches underfoot, my own movements creating echoes in the dark. But the prickling sensation of being watched flooded over me.

Hands trembling, I quickened my pace. Walking in these woods at dusk was foolish. If I fell here alone, no one would find me for days.

I thought bitterly of the life insurance.

"Ow!"

Suddenly, a thin branch slashed across my cheek, sharp and unexpected. I yelped, startled, raising my hand to find it wet and stinging.

Blood.

No longer just a man wary of predators—I was vulnerable, bleeding, an easy target.

I squinted through the failing light, wary of every shadow, every creak in the underbrush. Anxiety bloomed inside me like a dark flower.

What was I thinking? Was the life insurance money the only thing that made me feel valuable?

Worth more dead than alive.

I stopped and shivered, wondering how I had become this man—once ambitious and hopeful, now trapped in a cycle of half-hearted days spent in front of screens with Joey parked in front of the TV.

What had happened to my passion? To my wife's trust? To us?

That's when I heard it—the unmistakable crunch of leaves, purposeful and close.

I squinted into the gloom. "Who's there? Show yourself!"

My voice sounded hollow, fragile in the vast quiet.

I was an easy catch, standing out in the open, alone, and afraid.

The woods held their breath.

A desperate urge to hide seized me—was it some primal instinct clawing its way up?

My body responded without thought. I crouched low, though not as easily as in my twenties, and pressed on, skimming the unstable earth as quickly and quietly as it would bear me.

The cold chilled the air, the temperature dipping further, yet sweat beaded along my skin, dampening my palms, making my grip slippery and uncertain.

I had lost my way.

Completely, utterly lost.

I once felt like I was a part of the land, moving through the woods as if I were a child of the trees and shadows. But that was then, in the innocent daylight.

Now? Now I was trespassing in a living nightmare I'd foolishly invited on myself.

"Ah!" The cry burst from my lips—not for pain, but surprise —as my foot caught on something hidden beneath dead leaves.

I crashed down, arms shooting out instinctively to protect myself. My body tumbled over a cluster of jagged rocks; soft flesh met unyielding stone with bruising impact.

My foot jammed painfully between two rocks, momentum toppling me like a rag doll.

Lying there, I tasted silence, cold biting through my clothing, heart hammering wildly.

Then—again.

Crunch.

A sound too deliberate, too close. Ten feet away. I rolled over, struggling to sit upright, straining to pierce the black embrace of night.

My childhood home spread before me, distorted into a maze of menacing shadows. The trees I once climbed, the rocks I'd dashed over—they now melded into dark hulks where a predator could lurk unseen.

A mountain lion. That made sense. Silent. Watchful. Eyes gleaming like molten gold, waiting for the moment I buckled.

I forced myself up, every muscle screaming protest. Eyes locked on the source of the noise, searching for the faintest sign of movement. Figures lurked—dark and still—but I caught whispers of motion to the left and right.

Panic surged alongside a spark of fury.

I edged past jagged stones, scrambling onward. There was a path. I'd trod it countless times before. If I could reach it, I could find my way back to the car.

To safety. To sanity.

I don't want to die.

But—do I? Part of me wondered, bitter and raw—would the release even be welcome in a life weighed down by judgment and regret? Life's sweetness had soured, my soul tasting ash.

I tasted something familiar.

Fear.

That unmistakable cocktail—body slick with clammy sweat, armpits sour and tight. It wrapped around me, chilled and suffocating.

I was terrified. No shame in admitting it.

With the shadows closing in, the world pitching beneath me, branches slashing at my face—they told me fear sharpened senses, lit a fire under muscle and mind.

Up ahead, a dim opening between trees hinted at the path. The sparse tree trunks framed a clearing—was this my salvation? But which way to step? Left? Right?

Crunch.

The noise came again—on my right. Without hesitation, I turned left. My breath rattled as I glanced back; black shapes remained, relentless and close.

Something deeper than fear stoked my heart—rage. There was a presence here, unseen and cruel, toying with my mind, daring me to break.

I dropped low by the path's edge, frantically feeling the dirt for a stick, a rock—anything to defend myself. My fingers trembled over twigs and pebbles. Why hadn't I brought a knife? Even Tarzan carried one.

Crunch! Crunch! Crunch!

Closer—approaching fast. My hands shook. No weapon. Just raw panic cresting like a wave.

I leapt up and fled, thorns shredding my clothes—were they claws? Was it running beside me, ahead, behind? I couldn't tell.

"H-Help!" The sound tore from my throat, ragged and gasping.

"HELP!" Louder this time, desperation bleeding through.

I could almost taste its breath, hot and fetid, on my skin. Sharp teeth bared, eyes blazing with a savage hunger.

Ahead, a clearing. If I reached it, maybe lights, a road—life.

But my legs betrayed me—rubbery and weak.

My lungs wheezed, my heart thundered at the edge of bursting.

Just a few more steps...

Branches blocked me. I stopped dead.

I stood at the cliff's edge.

A sheer drop cradled in shadow.

Years forgotten, this deadly boundary marked the border of my childhood property—a place we never dared explore.

I peered down. Lights twinkled in the valley far below, calm and oblivious to my terror.

Here was my terrible choice: tumble into death's embrace, or linger and face the unseen horror behind me.

Two hundred fifty thousand dollars.

My lungs burned. I sank to my knees at the precipice, barely able to breathe.

All they would ever need—all it would take—was for me to die.

"No," I whispered hoarsely, lifting my gaze to the heavens.

Overhead, a tapestry of stars stretched vast and infinite.

"I want to live," I breathed, trembling. "I WANT TO LIVE!"

Fingers brushed a smooth stone. I grabbed it, standing unsteadily, heart pounding defiance.

I faced the woods—waiting.

Silence.

Then—

Crunch.

The steps moved closer.

"I'M READY FOR YOU!" I shouted, voice cracking but fierce. The rock weighed heavy in my hand, a paltry weapon against the dark.

"Hello?" a soft voice called.

My arm dropped. The stone slipped free, thudding against dirt.

"Who's there?" I challenged, voice steadier than I felt.

"I'm here to help. Are you alright?"

A beam of light sliced through the black, sweeping toward me.

"I'm here!" I answered, stepping into the glow.

"Careful," the voice warned gently. "That cliff's a nasty drop."

"Yes," I choked back tears, moving toward the figure. "Are you a ranger?"

"I know these woods."

His silhouette loomed large and steady beside me.

"You gave me quite a scare," I admitted. "Following me like that."

He chuckled softly. "I heard you call out. Lost out here at night?"

"Yeah. I parked in the main lot," I said, voice small.

"I'll walk you back."

"Please." Relief flooded me as the flashlight beam stretched ahead, weak but guiding.

The woods whispered and shifted as we moved. His light flickered faintly, casting a greenish hue.

"Nice of you to help," I muttered, craving conversation.

"These woods can swallow you in the dark," he replied.

"I used to live here, once," I said, eyes tracing familiar but threatening shapes.

"You did?"

"Yeah. Played these forests as a kid. But tonight… I took a wrong path. Tried to reach Indian Rock."

"The arrowheads?"

"Right. You know about that?"

He nodded. "Not much escapes me out here."

"Really?"

"These woods are special. The old ones—"

"Old ones?"

He hesitated. "The Native Americans. This is where they'd begin vision quests."

His voice held reverence, pulling memories from the shadows of my mind.

"Vision quest?"

"They came here troubled, building sweat lodges and walking long days. Spirits would come—sometimes beasts, sometimes animals, guiding them."

"Spirits?"

"Yeah. Sometimes fierce. Sometimes gentle."

I shivered, unsure if it was the story or the lingering darkness beyond the light.

We walked in silence, the forest settling around us.

His bulky frame moved beside me, unknown beneath the night.

Ahead, the soft outline of my minivan shimmered—a beacon.

He flashed the light in my eyes.

"So—what did you learn?" he asked.

"What?"

"Started in the circle of rocks. You've walked."

"How'd you know that?"

"Seems you had your own vision quest."

I swallowed memories and fear. "Someone—some *thing* followed me... I was afraid it would kill me. Maybe... maybe I wasn't sure if I wanted to live."

"And now?"

I smiled. "I do, I definitely want to live."

"A valuable lesson," he said quietly. "Hope it helps."

The flashlight sputtered—

Darkness swallowed us.

"Hey?" I called shakily.

But the shadow, taller than me, was gone.

The full moon rose, cold and silver, flooding the field and illuminating the path beneath my feet.

My minivan sparkled in the moonlight.

"Where'd you go?" I whispered.

I was alone.

Truly alone for the first time that night.

The hair on my neck rose. My heart slammed.

He was never there.

Adrenaline surged anew. I stumbled to the van, fumbling keys, trembling fingers unlocking safety.

I slid inside, threw the engine to life, and tore away, headlights off until the glare of the main road blinded me.

Home.

When I got there and stumbled in the door, my wife's eyes widened, seeing me. "My God, you look like you've seen a ghost."

"I might have," I replied, pulling her close. Grateful beyond words for her warmth, for the tether to life.

She tended my wounds with gentle hands, bathing away fear alongside blood.

"Where were you? You're all cut up."

"Got lost," I confessed.

She drew a soaking bath. I sank into the tepid water, clutching a stiff drink.

She wrapped my ankle, pressed tender bandages to bruises.

"Things are going to be different," I promised, tears spilling free.

She glanced worried. "Honey?"

"No," I said, voice breaking. "I'm done wasting my life. I'll help like you asked. I'll finish that book. I won't let fear steal me anymore."

"You're shaking."

"I realized: I don't want to die."

She traced fingers through my hair. "Nobody wants that."

"I need to work, to live something worthy."

I pulled her close, kissing away despair.

She took my hand, drawing me to the bed.

That night, we made love—fierce and urgent, igniting a fire extinguished too long.

For the first time in years, I felt alive.

I never told her what happened that night—not in detail, not ever. Part of me still isn't sure what really happened.

All I know is that when death stared me down, every trivial worry I'd carried suddenly seemed insignificant—like dust swirling in a vast, indifferent wind.

Afterward, things shifted. Whoever—or whatever—was there with me, it offered a glimpse of a bigger picture, something beyond the daily grind and petty fears that consumed me.

The small stuff—the arguments, the deadlines, the endless chores—none of it seemed to matter anymore. Somehow, I found solace in the rhythm of cleaning the house. The steady motion helped quiet my mind, and in that quiet, stories flowed.

I started writing again. A lot. Stories, initially short ones, came pouring out, as if the doorway to my creative mind had opened widely.

Then I returned to the novel I'd abandoned months ago, and this time it felt different. It wasn't perfect; it probably wouldn't be the 'Great American Novel' anyone expected, but to hell with that.

Writing felt like a gift I nurtured. Each word was a small victory, a proof that I was still here, still alive in more than just breathing.

That summer, we took Joey out for a picnic at the farm. The warmth of the sun kissed the meadow where Joey happily chased butterflies, his laughter drifting through the breeze like a fragile melody.

I felt a restless pull and slipped away from the group, wandering into the woods with an almost magnetic certainty. The path to Indian Rock was clear beneath the dappled sunlight, as if the forest itself was guiding me.

I'd done some digging into the old tales—the vision quest, the sacred rituals that depended on the guides you find and the lessons you receive.

I wanted to honor that somehow, to leave behind something worthy of the place. So, I gathered sticks, yarn, and even some feathers I'd carefully collected from a vulture exhibit at the zoo, crafting a small dreamcatcher.

Not much, but carrying with it a hope—that it might bring peaceful dreams, true visions, or perhaps a sign of gratitude from the unseen.

I placed it carefully in the center of the stone circle, my fingers lingering over the rough edges.

A quiet tension filled me, a fragile hope mingling with the fear that I was intruding on something ancient and profound.

Did whatever watched over this place accept my humble offering? Would it watch over me, too? As I stepped back into the shadows of the trees, I carried that question with me, unspoken but heavy as the forest air.

The Traveler

I tend to write long short stories and even longer books. But I wanted to challenge myself and do some 'flash fiction' that would only be about a thousand words. The little tale came to me in the Juneau, Alaska airport.

The Traveler

He turned the page slowly, eyes flicking up to the clock mounted above the terminal gates—an old-fashioned analog with sweeping hands and bold numbers.

Two hours remained before his flight.

Joe sat alone in the cramped Juneau airport terminal, Alaska's chill drifting through the glass doors. A quick hop to Seattle, then home to Janine. The thought steadied him.

He closed the dog-eared paperback resting on his knee and exhaled. Forty years of marriage had sculpted Janine into a woman who defied time's dulling touch—she still carried the spark of youth despite years spent raising children and weathering the storms of middle age.

Retirement loomed ahead like a promised oasis.

Joe longed for it. Longed to stop moving, to stop saying goodbye too often.

But the Juneau account was critical. Important enough that Joe had insisted on handling it in person, dragging himself across the country to Alaska's remote edge. He needed this flight.

Reaching into his jacket pocket, Joe searched for the familiar crinkle of paper—his boarding pass.

Empty.

A cold twist clenched his gut. He patted every pocket again—watch, keys, wallet, nothing but fabric. He rose, heart thudding, eyes scanning beneath and behind the padded chair, the small table next to him.

Nothing.

Frantic now, he patted down his other pockets—still no boarding pass. Then—his phone. A sinking feeling. That was missing too.

Joe's mind raced. Did someone rob him? Pickpocketed in the sterile terminal?

He struggled to remember anyone suspicious along the way, anyone who'd brushed too close. Nothing. No faces attached to the threat.

He forced himself down the escalator to the terminal's first floor, stepping briskly to the nearest kiosk. Fingers trembling, he typed his name.

A blip. Then the cruel message:

THIS REQUEST DOES NOT MATCH ANY RECORDS.

He blinked, disbelief washing over him. He entered his name again. And again.

Same result.

His breath hitched. Janine's face blurred before him—her warm smile waiting at the baggage carousel. How disappointed she'd be if he didn't arrive. She insisted on driving him herself, refusing the limo the company had offered, saying she wanted to be the first face he saw after a long journey.

He tried to push the panic down.

No boarding pass, phone or baggage tag. He had no memory of checking-in. In fact, he couldn't even recall how he'd arrived in the terminal.

A fog thickened in his mind.

He approached the customer service desk, where a young woman with wavy brown hair looked up from her screen.

Her smile dimmed the moment she saw him.

"Excuse me," Joe said, voice tight. "I seem to have lost my boarding pass."

She nodded curtly. "Yes, Mr. Hodges. Let me get my supervisor."

"How do you know my name?" Joe blurted, alarm rising.

She looked uncomfortable, forcing a polite smile. "I just... I'll call my superior."

Before long, a gray-haired woman appeared, her face drawn tight, eyes wary.

"Mr. Hodges. Good to see you, sir," she said, her tone clipped but nervous.

Joe frowned. "Do you know me?"

"Of course," the woman said, voice low. "I'm afraid they canceled your flight."

The words hit Joe like a blow.

"It can't be. Look," he said, gesturing toward the departure board listing the flight in bright letters. "It's right there!"

"Please lower your voice, Mr. Hodges," she cautioned.

"I need to get on that flight. My wife is waiting for me."

"Mr. Hodges," the woman hesitated, "we can arrange transport back to your hotel."

"I don't want to go back," Joe snapped, surprising even himself with his sudden flare of anger. "I need that flight—"

Two uniformed security officers appeared, one young and uneasy, the other larger and calm.

"Is there a problem here, Mr. Hodges?" the older officer asked.

Joe whirled, eyes blazing. "How do you know my name?"

The officer's gaze was steady. "They canceled your flight, Mr. Hodges. We've arranged a car to take you to your hotel."

"No! I want to fly home. I lost my phone, and my wife… she'll be waiting."

The officer's expression softened. "You can call her from the hotel, sir."

Reluctantly, Joe allowed himself to be guided toward the door, arm clipped gently by the officer.

Outside, a small white van waited, its sides emblazoned with the words 'Shady Rest.'

The driver, dressed in plain white, opened the passenger door.

"Well, I'm not happy about any of this," Joe muttered, sliding into the back seat.

"We'll call your wife, Mr. Hodges," the driver assured as the door shut behind him.

Frustration coiled tight within Joe as the van pulled away from the terminal. Through the metal screen separating them from the driver, his eyes narrowed.

Inside the terminal, the younger officer turned to his superior, voice low. "What's his story?"

The older man sighed, rubbing his temple. "Joe Hodges. Came through here on business last year. Got terrible news and snapped—violent enough that the state had to commit him. Now, every so often, he shows up here convinced he's about to board a flight home. The asylum sends a car to pick him up."

The young officer's eyes widened. "What kind of news?"

"His wife," the senior man said quietly. "She died in a car accident on the way to pick him up. Before his plane even left the ground."

The van hummed through the roads, carrying a man trapped between memory and reality—longing for a journey that no longer existed.

Into The Abyss

Based on a concept by Marvin Kaye

I created this Halloween horror story for the anthology *The Ultimate Halloween*. Marvin Kaye was looking for stories to fill out his anthology and asked if I was interested in writing one.

"What should it be about?" I asked.

"What do you do during Halloween?" was his reply.

"Well, as a professional entertainer and performer," I responded. "I usually spend a lot of time wearing different makeup."

He considered this for a moment, then said, "That's good. You should write about that!"

This led to my story about a makeup artist who was a little too good, and the job offer of a lifetime...

Into The Abyss

....

One

The creature walked to the door and brought its huge green hands to the lock. Flat black fingernails reflected darkly as its hands inserted and turned the keys. The elongated forehead pulsed with the concentration of the task until finally the door came open.

The tall green figure made a noise somewhere between a snarl and a sigh, exhausted by its quest. It walked into the room with the unsteady gait of a reanimated corpse, shabby clothes clinging to the tall shoulders.

Something was wrong.

It walked to the dining room table and found the note. The clumsy fingers opened the envelope and pulled the piece of paper free. This left dark-green fingerprints, as if its very flesh was sloughing off, decomposing.

It held the note close to its face.

Stan;

**I've had it! This is NOT what I bargained
for when we moved in together.**

**I thought we were 'ACTORS', but you've
sold out. I can't take what you've become—or
the mess. I'm moving in with a friend from
work.**

Don't try to find me

Julie

The creature's mouth opened.

"Damn," Stanley Nathan said aloud.

He put the note down and walked to the bathroom. She was right; it was a mess. Half-open bottles of spirit gum, ripped toilet paper, and coagulated droplets of liquid latex decorated the sink, commode, and tub.

He took off the overlarge coat, with the huge shoulder pads sewn into the decaying yoke, and bent to loosen the shoes with the enlarged heels. He pulled off the rope belt, the shabby pants, and the turtleneck shirt as he turned on the shower.

Reflected in the mirror, it was a startling contrast: the pale pink skin of his chest and arms and the green on his hands. He stepped under the hot spray and picked up a bottle of baby oil, rubbing the liquid on his face and hands. The "crypt green" greasepaint came loose and ran like blood down the drain.

Carefully and systematically loosened the rubber forehead as the oil relaxed the adhesive, he removed the headpiece—complete with toupee—from his own head, uncovering his thinning hair with the strong widow's peak..

Soaping himself, he used several makeup removers to turn himself from a movie-perfect reproduction of the Frankenstein monster back into plain old Stanley Nathan.

She really did it. I can't believe it!

When he and Julie moved to New York from Ohio intending to become actors, they arrived with very little, except love. Now they didn't even have that. A year in the big, bad city and she did three showcases and held a job as a waitress.

Stanley used his talent with makeup to perform at parties. Not small parties, but the fanciest ones in town, where hosts spent gobs of money for a night of privileged pleasure. He could become anyone, from movie stars to an accurate recreation of the Grinch. He cast his own prosthetic rubber pieces and was in demand by more and more of the best party planners in Manhattan.

And this was his season: Halloween.

Here on October 30th, he was returning from a party aboard the Intrepid, with people dining on caviar and champagne. Stanley met the guests at the door, unmoving as a mannequin.

"Doesn't that look real!" one woman, dripping in diamonds, said.

"Thank you," Stanley replied in his best Boris Karloff, causing the woman to shriek, first with terror and then laughter.

He was at that party for two hours. He would get a check for it that could easily cover the monthly rent of the small one-bedroom apartment in the part of town called 'Alphabet City'. The one he had shared with Julie until this evening.

He got out of the shower and dried himself.

"She's just jealous," he said aloud, meeting his own eyes in the mirror. "Jealous that I got so good with the makeup."

Eyes ringed with green stared back, coupled with a look of doubt that surprised him.

He pulled out a pad of eye makeup remover and wiped the last of the green from his pores. The expression of doubt remained.

Getting into bed, every muscle ached from the stiff pose he'd assumed and from all the nights previous. But his mind wouldn't shut down.

He'd spent the month working almost every day: Frankenstein at one party, Dracula at another, even portraying a stunning hunchback at one event, his face distorted grotesquely, with a glass eye sticking out from a fake rubber brow.

Julie's departure didn't completely surprise him. Arguments started once the party planners began calling regularly, and each job this month made the tension grow.

"You're too good for this!" she told him, her pretty face still clear in his mind. "It's just dressing up shit! You could do real acting. You're selling out!"

The image of her face stayed with him until he fell asleep.

Two

The phone woke him the next morning.

"Julie, can you get that?" Stanley yelled, but her side of the bed was empty. Then he remembered and stumbled out to the other room to grab the phone, cursing when he stubbed his toe.

"That's a nice way to talk to someone giving you work!" The woman's voice graveled by too many cigarettes. It was Annette Freling, one of his top party planners, who booked only high-class events.

"What? Oh, Annette! I'm sorry, I hit my foot," Stan muttered, still not awake. "What time is it?"

"Eight thirty, bubby!" Annette said, with as much of an apology in her voice as she was capable of. "I realize this is an early call, but I had to find out if you were busy."

Stan opened the pages of his datebook, rubbing his eyes with his free hand, trying to bring them into focus.

"Sure, what date?"

"Tonight!" Annette snapped.

"Tonight?"

"As in tonight, Halloween! I got a call from someone with a lot of money. I told them that you were probably booked."

"No, I'm clear," Stanley said, as he gazed with surprise at his calendar. It was odd that he had nothing tonight of all nights. In the days leading up to the big night, he'd had events, but All Hallows Eve was available.

"You're kidding!" Annette shrieked. "Oh my God, this guy really is the luckiest sonofabitch on the planet."

"Who?" Stanley asked, beginning to wake up.

"Michael Baal, the guy who's rebuilding half of Manhattan and owns the other half, that's who! I got a call from his office. God forbid he should pick up a phone—"

"Isn't that guy richer than Bloomberg, but no one ever sees him?"

"People see him, just not lowly rabble like us. His guy—Mr. Austere, if you can believe it—called from his office, and I think I can book you!"

"Tell me about it. What do they want? Frankenstein? Maybe the Wolfman?"

"No, tzatskelah. Mr. Austere said they wanted someone who was an expert. They want something special, a custom makeup."

"Christ, Annette. It takes days to do a custom job."

"Listen to me, Stanley," Annette croaked. "This is a special situation. Baal has this nightclub—it's only open one night a year, tonight."

"Then why did he wait until the last minute?" Stan muttered.

"The point is, he wants what he wants and usually gets it. Money is no object."

"What does that mean?"

"It means I'll double your last custom job."

Stanley held still for a moment. His last specialty design netted him enough to keep him going for months. And with Julie gone, he would now pay all the bills.

"I can't give you an answer until I see what they want," Stanley said, covering his options.

"It was just e-mailed to me. Can I send it along to you?"

"Okay. I'll call you back as soon as I figure out if I can even do it."

"You can do it. You're the best! I'll send it right away." Her excitement stimulated a coughing fit, and Stanley held the phone away from his ear until it passed.

"I'll speak to you soon," Stanley said and hung up. He walked into the kitchen and started coffee, then booted up his laptop—the one he'd paid for the night he'd gotten the $600.00 tip.

Julie was jealous. She had never made that kind of money as a waitress.

I have a talent; I use it, and I take pride in what I can do. There's nothing wrong with that!

But he knew he was justifying his position. Had he sold out, like she said?

He opened his e-mail and opened the message marked AAA MOST IMPORTANT.

It was a very odd illustration. It looked like artwork that might have graced the cover of an old magazine like Heavy Metal.

A demon—but not just any demon—it was an amazingly well-crafted fallen angel with a bald head, slight bumps that suggested horns, an exaggerated chin, and brilliant yellow eyes.

Stanley whistled and leaned back in his chair. The overall effect was stunning. He expected the demon to be half naked with rippling muscles, but it was in a fine tuxedo, looking extremely fashionable and attractive in an otherworldly way.

Stanley looked away from the image. The eyes were so intense; they seemed to burn into his soul. Hitting 'print', his printer buzzed and whirred, and he looked again at the likeness on the screen, trying to remain the observer.

He studied the facial structure to see if it would fit his face: the long chin; he'd need a new nose; the horns looked easy enough, more like knobs than what an animal might have.

He opened another program as the printer worked. It contained a drawn image of his face that he could alter with different additions. The software was based on what police sketch artists use, though not as sophisticated. It would only add things to the central figure—his own. He couldn't reduce his chin size or placing his eyes. Stanley found it a very useful tool to plan out a makeup before he started casting appliances.

He added a fake chin, stretching it to a new length, and then adjusted the brow of the head, and the nose.

He grabbed the finished rendition from the printer and placed it next to the computer screen. He made a few more changes. After a half-hour, he called Annette.

"So, bubby, what's the story?" she asked hoarsely.

"I can, but it's a lot of work. You need to triple that last job —"

"Triple? Are you out of your mind?"

"Annette, you said money was no object. If I'd gotten this a week ago, double would have done it, but I have to do it in one day. Just making the molds would normally take two days. As it is, I have to do the molds and cast the pieces today!"

"I know, but—"

"Frankly, there isn't a makeup artist outside of Hollywood that can do this, so that's the deal. If it's me, it's triple."

"Give me ten minutes," she murmured, and the line went dead.

Stanley hung up the phone and looked at his printed version of the demon. He could do the yellow eyes; he already had a pair of contact lenses that were darn close. The bald head could be done with a Woochie brand headpiece, of which he had several already cut to fit. The red makeup would easily cover the hair underneath the bald cap better than a flesh tone would, and he had red greasepaint, though he couldn't be sure of a perfect match.

Making a list of what he already owned and what he had to cast, he printed up the computer sketch of his face with the additions.

He was excited and wanted to do this job, even though it was a hell of a lot of effort. It would be his best work to date.

The phone rang. It was Annette.

"You got it, bubby! Jeez, I can't believe it. I'll have you know, I'm making nothing on this."

"I appreciate it," Stanley said. Annette claimed this every time she booked him, but he knew for a fact that she made a fine commission from everyone who worked through her.

She gave him the address of the club, a converted downtown warehouse on Tenth Avenue.

"What time do I start?"

"Ten PM, and you go to midnight. That's all," she said, and chuckled. "Damn fine money for two hours' work! And you didn't even have to sell your soul!"

Stanley raised his head and stared into the eyes of the demon on the paper before him.

"What makes you say that?" Stanley wondered, inexplicably troubled.

"It's just an expression, tzatskelah," Annette croaked.

"Of course," Stanley replied. Why did it bother him? "What's the place called?"

"Here's the best part. Get this, it's called The Abyss."

Three

The rest of the day was a blur of activity. He called upon all the expertise he'd mastered since his arrival in New York. He used clay and sculpting tools to mold the chin, nose, and forehead on a plaster cast of his face he already owned. It took over two hours, but the results matched the distinct look of the illustration.

He then mixed a rapid-setting plaster of Paris. Carefully using dams to separate the head into three sections, he cast the pieces of his demonic re-creation.

It was necessary to wait at least an hour to make sure the plaster cured completely. So, he spent the time finding his yellow contact lenses, the bald cap, and the latex foam mix.

The rubber-based chemicals were easy to use, but tricky. The trouble was, it had to cure completely in a specially built box outside Stanley's window. It was now after noon, and full curing would take several hours.

"Damn lucky I don't start until ten," Stan said, as he carefully took the solid plaster molds off the face. He then took his smaller sculpting pick and removed chunks of clay that remained within the mold.

Soon Stan had three sets of clean molds. He put a releasing agent into each one and mixed the equal measures of latex goo and reagent. This had to be done thoroughly and with care as he observed the mixture for signs of the reaction.

He placed the individual molds into a sizable wooden box that lay on the fire escape. Built by a friend, this box contained a heating element and fans. Plugging in the power cord, he closed the window, and stepped away from the curing rubber.

"Now, it's just a matter of time. It either worked or it didn't," he said aloud to the room. His last custom job required him to cast each facial piece two or three times to create pieces that met his requirements. But in this case, if the product wasn't right, he wouldn't have time to cast another set.

Sitting down, he turned on the television and tried to relax.

My best work to date, Stanley thought, *if it all comes out.*

At eight o'clock, Stanley stood in his bathroom in his underwear and T-shirt. The first thing he did was slip in the yellow contact lenses while he had clean hands.

Studying the facial pieces, he put a final coating of castor oil and greasepaint on each section. They turned out perfectly, and

Stanley knew it the minute he gently separated each piece from its mold with bated breath and clenched teeth.

This was the moment that excited him most, when he would attach the lifeless rubber to his face and make it appear to be living tissue. It gave him a thrill akin to what Dr. Frankenstein felt when the lifeless corpse stirred.

Starting with the bald cap, he applied the spirit gum to the skin around his hairline and used the blow dryer to speed the process.

He then picked up the brow, its small, stubby horns protruding. As he watched himself in the mirror to see where each piece would fit on his face, and put spirit gum in the proper places. Then, he carefully attached the headpiece, erasing the edges with liquid latex and a stipple sponge.

Proceeding down the face, he affixed the nose and was especially careful with the chin. He would talk and laugh with the patrons at the nightclub, and if it was too close to his mouth, the rubber piece could work loose.

"Magic time," he said as he grabbed the greasepaint. He touched the rubber with quick little pats and softly rubbed the makeup on all his exposed flesh, as well as on the back of his neck.

He looked in the mirror. Gone were the streaks of different colored skin and rubber. His complexion was uniformly red. The face staring back at him with yellow eyes was so startling, his breath caught.

"Jesus!" he said, as the demon in the mirror moved its lips with his. "I got it! I got it dead on!"

He went to the doorway and called out, "Julie, you have to see this—"

He stopped at the threshold, as he remembered she was gone.

"Stupid!" he spat. "She'd rather work as a waitress. Look what I can do!"

He returned to the image in the mirror, now even more animated, and for a moment, Stanley couldn't figure out why. He slowly realized his anger made the face even more alive.

Alive and evil.

After powdering the makeup and brushing off any excess, he dressed in his good white shirt and tuxedo. He knew the red greasepaint might never come out of the collar, but after tonight, he could buy extra shirts. Dozens if he wanted.

As a final touch, Stanley washed his hands and picked up red airbrush makeup, which he applied to his wrists. He knew from the drawing that he would wear gray gloves, but he wanted to make sure that any exposed skin matched his face.

A last-minute inspiration struck him, and he pulled out a short black cape with a red lining he used for Dracula a week earlier.

He went outside and walked down to Fourteenth Street to catch the crosstown bus. It was a little after nine, and there were people out on the cool autumn night. They looked at him, but they didn't point and laugh, like when he was Frankenstein or even the Hunchback. People stared, but their faces were grim— even frightened.

He got on the bus and swiped his Metrocard. The bus driver, a black man, looked up, his eyes wide.

"Good evening!" Stanley said in a deep voice.

"Uh, evening. Man, you look—" the driver said and stopped mid-sentence. He tried to smile but could not.

Stanley sat, the other patrons giving him a wide berth.

This is a sense of power unlike anything I've ever experienced.

It was thrilling.

Four

Stanley arrived at the club at nine-forty, and as he approached, he saw a long line of partygoers in costumes. They were beautifully and expensively garbed. Some wore makeup, but nothing at the level of his skill.

And Stanley knew it.

Two men standing at the door drew his attention because of their size. They were huge, bigger than any bouncers he'd ever seen. And each wore a large demon head with impressive horns.

Must be a Celastic molded head resting on the guy's shoulders, Stanley decided.

They were excellent designs, as the eyes seemed to follow his every movement.

He moved past the roped area and right toward the door. He expected to be stopped by the two goons, but as he approached, they bowed and stood aside.

Of course, they're expecting me.

As he walked into the lobby, a man standing in the corner stared up at him. He wore glasses and a suit and looked like he'd dressed up as a nerd accountant for Halloween.

He approached Stanley, sweat beaded on his brow, his mouth moving, but no words came out until he was right next to Stanley.

"S-sir, I—I—" he sputtered, his face blanching.

"Good evening," Stanley said in his deep voice. "I'm Stanley Nathan. Who do I see to find out where I'm performing?"

The man's thin face turned a bright shade of scarlet, almost matching Stanley's temporary skin hue.

"O-of course!" he blurted out. "I'm Austere, Mr. Austere. I'm the one who hired you. It's just that, well… the re-creation of what we sent. I mean, I was told you were good—"

"Thank you," Stanley said, proud of his work. Tonight was a crowning achievement, even if Julie ran out on him. If she could see him now!

Mr. Austere called over another man with a mustache and Van Dyke beard to murmur into his ear. The man nodded and approached Stanley, smiling.

"Sir, would you like to look around?"

Stanley nodded. "Please! By the way, what is this character called?"

"Called?" the man said, stopping short.

"Does he have a name? I mean, the drawing was so specific —"

"I don't know," the man said, becoming uncomfortable as he looked into Stanley's yellow eyes. "Satanic Majesty? Prince of Darkness? Anything you like."

"Prince," Stanley said. "I like that. Call me 'The Prince'!"

"As you wish. Please follow me."

They stepped through the door that separated the lobby from the large nightclub beyond. Stanley heard the rhythm of a heavy bass beat. He didn't really hear it so much as feel the pulse in the surrounding walls.

The man with the beard opened the door, and the music increased to the point of pain. A combination of metal rock and garbled lyrics that sounded like screams. Stanley realized the one thing he'd forgotten tonight was his earplugs.

As he entered, he completely forgot about his ears or the music. The main room was the most amazing display he'd ever seen. It was as if someone had taken an illustration of Dante's Inferno and brought it to horrific life in this one cavernous room.

There were several levels and dance floors, and in the center was a vast pit, which belched forth smoke with a hint of sulfur.

Nice touch!

Women wearing bat wings and very little else ran and jumped from level to level acrobatically. Their lithe forms moved with such wanton abandon, Stanley decided they must be expert gymnasts.

Chained figures stood along the walls, with stripes from whippings on their bare midriffs. The makeup was so stunningly real, Stanley thought he could sense the tinny scent of the blood.

His entrance caused a commotion among the winged women. They stopped and stared, then leapt and cavorted in his direction. The man with the beard stepped out in front of Stanley as the writhing swarm of women landed near him and fell into a huddled mass.

"Go on, all of you. This fellow is here as part of the show!" he bellowed, and Stanley could barely hear him above the music.

One woman, who seemed terribly young, yet far too experienced. She glanced at Stanley's crotch and licked her lips so lasciviously that he found it hard to breathe. Her eyes promised such possibilities.

The women tittered and giggled as the bearded man fretted. Finally, they moved away and returned to their perches throughout the room.

Stanley, freed from the temptress' glance, concentrated on the room. Every corner contained more than he expected. Realistic fires burned, and bodies shook in artificial torment on racks or hung from manacles. Of all the displays of macabre decor Stanley had ever seen, this was the ultimate.

Then his eyes fell on the chair at the highest point in the room. No, it couldn't be called a mere chair. A throne, a station of royalty and power! This would be a place for him to sit that night! A prince surveying the Kingdom of the Damned.

Stanley pointed at the chair. The bearded man grew pale and escorted him out to the lobby.

"That would be perfect—" Stanley was saying as they passed through the doors as they left the hellish din behind.

"I'm sorry, but that's the one place you cannot go," the man said firmly, but with an apologetic tone. "Not before midnight."

Stanley nodded, deciding that such a marvelous prop already had a purpose in the evening's festivities.

He glanced back at the room beyond the doors. "Quite a layout! And those women—"

"For your own safety, don't get too close. They'll eat you alive."

"What a way to go," Stanley sighed.

Mr. Austere appeared at Stanley's arm so suddenly that Stanley jumped.

"It's time to open the doors!" Austere said as he checked his watch.

"I'll greet people here to start off," Stanley replied in his character voice.

"That would be fine," Austere said, without meeting Stanley's eyes.

The doors opened, and the revelers came in slowly. Stanley thought it odd that no one collected a cover charge or checked IDs. They didn't even have invitations, but the bouncers, who wore the enormous heads, seemed to know who belonged and who didn't.

"Welcome to the Abyss! I am The Prince, your host," Stanley said, taking the job of the doorman. The reactions were much more varied than Stanley was used to. The makeup—that always impressed people. However, most of the guests seemed disquieted by his presence, only smiling when they saw inside the club.

After a half-hour at the door, Stanley wandered through the club. The music was still deafening and even more like screaming. The guests were extremely polite, offered him drinks and cigars, but were oddly reticent.

Still Stanley plugged on, shook hands, acknowledged the guests. He approached one of the winged women and danced with her, much to the girl's delight. He wanted to get close enough to see what she was really wearing. Could it be a body stocking with anatomical features airbrushed on?

Five minutes into the dance, and though he held her with gloved hands, he was sure she was not wearing a body stocking. Every bit of anatomy was gloriously hers. She wore little beyond a belt and leather contraption that covered her nether regions. The leather straps that went up over her shoulders and enclosed her nipples.

Even more confusing, he couldn't see the way the wings attached. At first glance, he'd assumed the leather straps held them in place. Instead, they seemed to be part of her flesh, attaching directly to her back.

Thinking about this, Stanley pulled her close to look past her shoulder and see what held them on. Without a word or gesture, the nymph fell to her knees, grabbed him by the waist, and nibbled at his crotch.

Stanley reeled back, and the creature leapt up, laughed, and ran off. Stanley looked around, thankful that the makeup covered any flush on his skin.

However, his dance partner was not the only one who indulged. There were couples... well... coupling... all over the room. On the dance floors or any free space they could find. Groups of two or three, men on men, women on top of each other. It was as if a bell had gone off and everyone was copulating with the nearest recipient with no concern for anything, least of all gender.

This is one of those nutty sex clubs!

The sight riveted Stanley; the lust of the scene enticed him. He felt an impulse to find his teasing dance partner and have his way with her.

Pulling himself out of the room, he went to the lobby to get some fresh air. He had to control himself as he was hired help, even if the club encouraged risqué behavior.

A tall, thin, bony man Stanley hadn't seen before ran up to him.

"Sir! Sir! It's almost midnight. You have to get to the—"

The man stopped talking as Austere came into sight and raised a hand.

"Relax, this is Mr. Nathan. He is an expert at makeup."

The thin man's face drooped, and his mouth fell open.

"Oh, sorry," he said, surprised and cowed by Austere. "I'll make sure everything is ready."

The thin man ran off. Austere approached Stanley.

"Everything all right, Mr. Nathan?"

"Yeah, it's just a little crazy in there," Stanley said, trying to catch his breath.

"Oh, it will be much crazier after midnight," Austere said, eyeing Stanley through his glasses. "Until dawn, I should think. Just be careful of the winged girls; they bite."

"So I've heard," Stanley said.

"That's why they wear the harnesses," he whispered hoarsely. "Because they bite *down there*."

Stanley realized that the straps and leather on the girls resembled, of all things, a muzzle.

Austere glanced at his watch and brought Stanley toward the door of the main room.

"Almost midnight. You'll want to see this!" Austere said.

They walked into the club just as a sound like thunder shook the air. People stood, broke apart from their partners, and looked up at the throne. A rumble came again, and flashes of light exploded about the room, with showers of sparks flying high into the air.

The people knelt as a figure rose from behind the chair.

This is going to be good!

A figure came forward, and the hairs on the back of Stanley's neck quivered, even glued down with rubber and spirit gum.

The figure looked just like Stanley in his makeup, but he projected such a presence that it filled Stanley with awe.

Standing tall, the demonic man stretched out his hand, and the people bowed, even Mr. Austere. Stanley felt compelled to bow as well.

"Do what thou wilt—" his voice boomed "—shall be the whole of the law!"

The kneeling figures let out a cheer, their voices raised in triumph. The demon sat on the throne, and with a flash of lightning, disappeared.

"Holy shit!" Stanley said as the guests cheered even louder. The music played again as buffet trays opened and couples continued where they left off.

Five

Austere pulled Stanley out toward the lobby and did not speak until they went through the door.

"If you don't mind, Mr. Baal would like to speak to you," he said as he led Stanley toward an elevator he hadn't noticed before.

"Sure," Stanley said, his head spinning. "I have to ask you, if you already had one guy in the makeup, what did you need me for?"

The elevator door opened, and Austere looked quizzically at Stanley, as if trying to absorb what he'd just said.

"Oh, you mean at midnight!" Austere said as the elevator rose. "That's an excellent question. This was—what do you call it? An audition of sorts. We have a great need for someone of your remarkable skills."

"Whatever for?"

"Mr. Baal would be the best person to answer that."

The elevator stopped with a soft "whoosh" and the door opened.

"Go in, Mr. Nathan. Mr. Baal is waiting for you."

"But I—"

"Just go, Mr. Nathan. I'll be there when you need me. I'm always nearby."

Stanley stepped out of the elevator and onto a carpet of such a deep, soft pile he felt as if he were floating. He was in a penthouse with the lights turned low, but ambient light entered through the many windows.

Stanley carefully walked forward, his eyes adjusting to the dim light of the room.

"M-Mr. Baal?" he said, just above a whisper.

A light came on, shining directly at him, blinding him. He lifted his hand to shield his eyes.

"No!" a man bellowed. "Lower your hand. I want to get a good look at you. Come closer."

Stanley lowered his hand and moved forward, unable to resist the sound of that voice. The light moved up and down Stanley's face for a good minute.

"Very nice!" the voice said. "Turn your head."

Stanley revolved his head one way, then the other.

"Excellent! Beyond my expectations. You, young man, are a genuine artist!"

"Thank you, sir," Stanley said. "After I saw the other fellow in makeup, I thought—"

"Other fellow?" the voice asked.

"Yes, on the throne. I thought he did a better job than I did —"

The voice broke into a hissing laugh that chilled Stanley.

"I imagine he looked better. Perhaps more realistic?"

"Yes, sir. I'm glad you still liked my work."

"Very much so!" the voice said. A shadowy figure lurked behind the light. "In fact, I want to hire you."

"Hire me?"

"To do this work for me—full time."

"You have more characters you want me to create?"

"No, just one character," the shadowy figure said. "In fact, it will be your finest work."

"Sir?"

The figure rose smoothly from the shadows, his silhouette cutting an imposing shape.

"I've always loved this time of year," he said, voice dripping with dark satisfaction. "It's the one day I can walk freely among my fellow creatures—without masks, without lies." He bent down and pressed a button on the ornate table.

Suddenly, the room flooded with light. Stanley blinked against the glare, turning to face the figure—and froze. It was as if he were staring into the bathroom mirror at home, yet this reflection chilled him to the bone. This was no mask, no greasepaint or rubber prosthetic.

It was the man's actual face.

Dread coiled tight in Stanley's stomach as he sank heavily into a nearby chair.

The demon's smile only widened. He moved to a small bar, poured two brandies with deliberate slowness, then handed a snifter across to Stanley. "Drink this. It'll warm you."

The warm burn of the brandy spread through Stanley's chest, but the icy knot in his gut remained.

"I am Michael Baal," the demon continued, voice low and smooth, "though that's merely my name for the world's consumption. I've built an empire—monuments of brick, steel, and power. But now," he leaned closer, eyes gleaming dangerously, "the public demands a face to match my creations."

Stanley's throat tightened. "No one's ever really seen you…" he whispered, staring at the flawless devil before him.

"Only a select few," Baal said, nodding to the side.

From nowhere, the lean figure of Mr. Austere materialized

"With your talents, Mr. Nathan, the world will finally see me." Baal's smile grew wicked. "Consider it your most challenging —and rewarding—assignment. If you can make yourself look like me, you can make me look… well, less conspicuous."

Stanley's voice barely rose above a whisper, trying to summon courage. "And if I refuse?"

Baal chuckled, the sound dark and endless. "But you won't, Mr. Nathan. You're too curious. Too proud of your craft. The challenge calls to you. I've sought someone with your skills for years."

The demon rose again, easing his lean form onto the edge of the desk. "You will travel with me. I will pay you handsomely— you've already glimpsed some of the fringe benefits tonight." His eyes glittered with promises and threats both.

A shudder ran through Stanley. The images came unbidden: the throng of writhing bodies, the wild abandon beneath the pulsing lights downstairs. He glanced up at Baal—calm, confident, inscrutable.

In his mind, Julie's voice echoed sharply, *You've sold out.*

Annette's croak followed, *You didn't even have to sell your soul!*

Was that what this was? Selling out? Selling his very soul?

But then Stanley recalled the rush of power from tonight—electric, intoxicating. And here, in the presence of this creature, the power magnified beyond measure.

He looked again at Baal's face—the angles, the unnatural perfection. If he could cover the horns with a wig, hide the chin's beneath skillful prosthetics and flesh-toned paint…

Before he knew it, Stanley was on his feet, stepping closer. He peeled off his gloves and tentatively touched one of the fleshy knobs jutting from Baal's forehead. The demon neither flinched nor withdrew.

"You want me to make you blend into any crowd? To hide behind the face of anyone you choose?" Stanley asked, voice rough with disbelief.

Baal's eyes burned like coals. "It would be your masterpiece."

Stanley cringed back from those eyes, but his mind overflowed with what Baal could give him, do for him. If he wanted to be an actor, Baal could arrange it. Money? Baal would supply it. Women? Ready and willing, like the ones downstairs.

All Baal asked, all he needed, was the one thing only Stanley could give him: a face.

"Yessss," Stanley breathed, sinking back into the chair, surrendering to the dark allure of the future laid before him.

Baal and Austere exchanged a knowing smile—their victory already sealed.

GHOST WRITER

A Supernatural Suspense Mystery

ARJAY LEWIS

MIND
BENDER
PRESS

Ghost Writer

I t was Franklin D. Roosevelt who said, "I think we consider too much the good luck of the early bird and not enough the bad luck of the early worm."

That day, I understood how that worm felt.

I've had plenty of bad days, but as I glared at Chandra — my second wife — across the court tables for our divorce proceedings, I felt it was just one more indignity piled on top of all the others.

I was hungover, and I couldn't even have a little of the hair of the dog, because they frown on you showing up in court with liquor on your breath.

Of course, this was the last step. Lawyers had parsed the details of our agreement as if it were of biblical origin. The lawyers investigated and deliberated over each sentence to find its true meaning.

Chandra's lawyer, the Shark, was there, smiling like she'd taken down Al Capone. My own ineffectual lawyer was there as well, a cordial enough man recommended by my publisher. On the first day of negotiations, the Shark had chewed him up and spat him out.

I bought a house ten years ago, restored it, and paid it off with my royalties and book advances, so I owned it free and clear.

Now after five years of marriage, my ex owned it free and clear.

The case was simple — it was the State of New Jersey. I possessed a penis; therefore, I must pay.

We had no children, so no child support. She accepted the house instead of alimony, accompanied by a large cash settlement, which dwindled my savings greatly.

I was currently living in a tiny cottage in a crowded neighborhood in Lake Hopatcong. One tiny bedroom, a bathroom with a shower stall, a minuscule living room, and a kitchen.

Not that I had much to put in it. All my good furniture stayed in the house that Chandra now owned.

Except my leather recliner. I had to have my recliner.

As she signed the divorce papers, Chandra looked up at me and winked.

I clenched my teeth so hard, it's a wonder I didn't crack a few of them. One more indignity.

I hated her, and at the same time, I desired her so badly it was surprising I didn't become aroused right there in the courtroom.

That was the thing with Chandra. She was bad for me. She was poison. All I had to do was see how she treated a waiter with her condescending attitude.

But, my God, the sex.

She was a fire I couldn't quench. I wanted her, and I wanted her badly. That was the one thing the divorce didn't change.

I drank to control my lust for her, especially as our marriage fell apart. She encouraged the drinking so that I would keep writing.

After all, you don't want to kill the golden goose, not until you receive a few more golden eggs.

Once the judge had approved the agreement, Chandra, me, and our lawyers stepped out into the hall to finish signing the paperwork

"You're off to your uncle's funeral," Chandra said as I finished signing. "Joe, give my best to the family. I always liked Rick. I'm sorry he died."

As a writer, I should have a great retort. Something worthy of Oscar Wilde, Mark Twain, or Dorothy Parker. But I wrote stories of spies, guys, and willing ladies. Lacking a comeback, I muttered, "Yeah, sure."

Brilliant! I missed my calling as a stand-up comedian.

She did like my Uncle Rick. He'd been beneficial to her, or at least to her plans. Richard Riley had been a renowned literary agent, and when I wrote stories as a child and teen, he encouraged me. We were a family of readers, and I was fortunate enough to grow up in the 80s and 90s when people still read books.

He helped me sell my short stories to magazines, and when I wrote my first novel, A Man Called Soul, he gave me excellent pointers and guided me to a content editor who brutally ripped the tale apart and had me rewrite it several times.

By the time of publishing, the book was so polished, it all but glowed.

Uncle Rick sold the book with a fair royalty for a new writer. I was thrilled, and taking my gains, I started the second book in what became a profitable series.

My lead character, Soul Mason, was a CIA agent helping to stop terrorists and evil plots. In the latter part of the 2000s, with terrorists as the bad guys, a brave, chisel-jawed CIA agent was just the sort of thing people wanted to read.

The second book in the series, Body And Soul, got me the money to buy my house, now the property of the ex-missus Riley.

She announced to me during our divorce negotiations that she would keep my last name. Since her maiden name was Crapanzano, I don't blame her. Riley is much easier to spell.

I left the Morris County Municipal Court a much poorer and bitter man, and my next port of call was Uncle Rick's funeral.

Chandra had been fond of Rick. She started working for him about six years ago as his assistant. I had dated no one seriously since my first marriage went bust before I sold my first novel.

That lasted only one short year. That must have been a long year for my ex, Elaine. I was a troublesome man to live with, struggling with my desire to write and my frustration at what I produced. I was an angry, sullen would-be writer.

There was no monetary settlement, and I remained in the New York City apartment we had shared.

Years later, once I was writing and sold some books, I got out of the city and bought the house. Six years ago, I showed up at Uncle Rick's office with a new book ready to go — and there was Chandra.

After six months of dating and the most mind-blowing sex I'd ever experienced, I proposed. We married a few months later and Chandra quit her job.

"I have to, Joe," she explained. "This way, I can help you with the next book. I'll fix your errors and help with the editing. I'll be your muse."

She was my muse alright, and I thought things were good, as we blissfully fornicated and she lubricated me with alcohol into a state of passivity.

But by the time I wrote Soul To The Devil, I realized my wife was living well beyond our means ,and I did not know where my money was going. She had taken over the finances so I could, as she put it, "focus on writing." Dummy that I am, at the time it seemed like a good idea.

It was about that time, six months ago, Uncle Rick informed me my book advances were going to be less.

The ebook revolution had gained momentum and was devastating the publishing industry. For years, the agents and publishers kept the riffraff at bay. But with the gatekeepers silenced, and the gates broken down, anyone could publish.

To the Stephen King's, the James Pattersons', and the Nora Roberts' this was no big deal. They were worth millions and their multi-million dollar advances, as well as the royalties, would keep rolling in. To a middle-of-the-list guy like me, it meant my income was going to go down.

I sobered up, figuratively and literally, and tried to figure out what happened to my money, which Chandra always referred to as "our money."

Which apparently meant "her money."

I moved out of my carefully restored house into a crummy little shack, hired a divorce lawyer and a forensic accountant, but they found little of the money. She siphoned it off slowly and cleverly, and boffed me into a state of unawares. Then she hired the Shark, who plucked my house and half my remaining savings.

The Shark argued I was still at the height of my productivity as a writer and would probably see much more money in the future. She said it was right to make a claim on future royalties as her client, "Was a vital part of the creation of Mr. Riley's very successful books."

Even my lame lawyer got that thrown out.

Of course, Chandra and the Shark knew something that my lawyer didn't. My latest book, tentatively titled Lost Soul, had netted me a small upfront advance, but I wouldn't get the rest until I delivered the book. In the past, I delivered a book or two after the requested deadline.

The due date for the latest book was two months away.

I had written exactly ten pages.

Chandra may have only been looking out for herself in our marriage, but she was correct: she was my muse. Her offerings of steady sex and booze kept me going, kept me working.

For the last few months, I'd done little writing.

All of this whirled through my mind as I arrived at the Stanley Funeral Home in a town called Clinton. It was a large, stately house, a Victorian converted for business use.

Uncle Rick's services were to be held in the largest room.

I arrived just as people were being called to sit down for the service. I saw my older cousins, Robert, Liam, and Ashley. Neither of my brothers came, which was fine by me. We had never been close, and they lived far away. Growing up, I was always closer to my cousins than my brothers. To the cousins, I was a fun visitor. To my brothers, I was the annoying baby of the family, and either a pain to deal with or someone to be bullied.

Walking in, I could see the open coffin at the front of the room. Uncle Rick looked as he did in life, a tall and lean man, around six foot-two with an excellent physique. His white hair gave him an air of maturity and wisdom. They had combed his hair neatly, and dressed him in one of his expensive suits; he looked ready to get up and take a meeting.

Uncle Rick was the last of that generation, as my parents died in a car accident when I was thirty-seven. Now, it was just me, my brothers, and my three cousins. That was all the family I had left.

But it wasn't like we all got together and hung out for the holidays.

I was still fighting a headache and wishing I had brought something with me to take a little nip, just to clear my head.

As I sat, a reverend spoke comforting words at the front of the room. From the gist of it, this eulogy could have been a prepared speech made from a template or thrown together by an AI program.

When he finished his opening tribute, he asked people to get up and talk about Rick.

Robert was the oldest son, so he rose and gave an excellent speech. I figured all those years working as a real estate salesman and investor gave him skills as a speaker.

When he finished, his younger brother Liam got up. Despite being in his late forties, Liam had yet to establish a solid foundation for his life. He was a chain smoker of cigarettes and pot, as well as imbibing in other substances, and squandered his nights away on alcohol and questionable company.

Not that I could judge, considering my ex-wife.

He constantly relied on others for money, with promises to pay them back that never came to fruition. I knew from experience, having given him about a thousand dollars by this point. I was smart enough to say it was a gift, because I knew there was no way in hell he'd ever pay me back.

Liam rambled his way through an unprepared speech, and all of us were thankful when he finished and sat.

My youngest cousin, Ashley, got up to speak, and to my surprise, she started reminiscing about summers in the Poconos in my uncle's rustic cabin. Growing up, all of us, my parents and brothers, my uncle Rick and aunt Betsy, and the cousins would all hang out for a couple of weeks there in the summer. Thinking back to all those people in the one cabin, I wondered how we all fit.

Whispering Pines.

That was the fanciful name Rick had given it.

Nestled in a national forest, the cabin stood out like a beacon among the towering trees. There were acres of woods and we had a dock on Sandy Rock Lake, large enough that we could swim and fish.

I recalled those times as she spoke. Memories of long-forgotten laughter and carefree summers flooded my mind, thoughts of sun-dappled days and warm nights.

From a young age, I looked forward to those annual trips to Uncle Rick's cabin.

It gave me a taste of life disconnected from the modern world. Back in the 90s, we didn't have screens and smart phones so we had to actually go outside and play, like kids are supposed to do.

All of us, brothers and cousins, slept in sleeping bags on the main room floor, while the adults had the two bedrooms.

I was the youngest of all my brothers and the cousins, and Ashley, like a little general, made sure the older boys included me in everything that was going on.

God, I adored her when we were kids, a mix of hero-worship and awe. She was six years older than me, with blonde hair and a powerful personality. We played games, roughhoused, and ran around those woods like little savages, all orchestrated by Ashley.

Then, as the sun dipped below the horizon, we would all gather around a crackling campfire. The adults shared stories as laughter echoed through the trees, and the scent of pine trees and freshly caught fish mingled with the aroma of wood smoke.

It was listening to these stories that made me want to be a writer, to tell stories to other people, and make them feel like I did on those nights.

My current life didn't have any of the peace or joy I felt when we stayed up in that cabin.

The service ending brought me back to awareness as everyone started getting ready to get into their cars and form a caravan to the burial site.

I just wanted to get a drink.

"Joey?"

I came around to see Ashley approach. She pulled me into a hug, the first hug I'd received from a woman in months.

"Hey, Ash," I said. "I'm so sorry."

She pulled back, and her short, chestnut-brown hair framed her face, her bright blue eyes wet. As usual, she dressed impeccably in a black pantsuit with a gray satin blouse. "At least it was quick. Not like Mom, slowly eaten away by the cancer. This was a shock, but it was almost easier."

I nodded sagely. What could I say? Is there ever a good way to die?

"Are you coming to the burial?" she asked.

"No, I've got other things," I said, avoiding the question as best as I could. "I divorced Chandra this morning."

Ashley's expression changed, and the tears were gone. "That bitch," she murmured. This was a stretch for my cousin, as she never used coarse language about anyone. "She took you for everything, didn't she?"

I lifted my shoulders in an attempt at a shrug. "She got the house."

Ashley shook her head, and I saw the fury in her eyes. My protective older cousin. She'd fought my battles as a child and looked like she would happily do it again. "I warned you about her. Didn't I tell you to get a prenup?"

I hung my head. "Please Ash. Today's been rough enough."

She put her hand under my face and lifted my chin. "All right, Joey. But don't be a stranger."

I nodded and forced a grin.

Other guests pulled her away, and a hand slapped me on the back. "Hey Joey."

My oldest cousin, Robert, pulled me into a bear hug. He was about fifty at that point, stocky with his dark hair showing traces of grey at the temples. He pulled back and looked at me. "You holding up alright, Joey? You look terrible."

"I divorced Chandra today," I said with a sigh.

"Ding-dong, the witch is dead," he murmured.

That got a grin. "Heard from her? I understand she called my brothers."

Robert shook his head. "She probably was looking for people to take her side. No, I was lucky enough not to be on her call list. How did you make out?"

"I got screwed, lost the house. My lawyer said if we went before a judge, I'd get screwed even worse. Her lawyer would portray me as a rich writer who was bad with money—"

He frowned. "I thought Chandra handled the money?"

"My first mistake. They'd make me look like a drunk kept solvent by my loving spouse, who deserved everything I owned because of my spendthrift ways." I shook my head.

Robert smiled his real estate agent smile. "I think we can help you take your mind off the situation. Come to the wake."

"Will there be food and booze?"

"An Irish wake?" He easily slipped into a fake brogue. "What else would ye have, Joey, me boy?" He dropped it and glanced around the room. "It'll be tonight at the Shamrock's Embrace Irish Pub right here in Clinton."

"Could they give it a more cliché name?" I asked.

"I would have gone with the Leprechaun's Asshole, but that's me," Robert grinned. "Look, I'm staying at the Holiday Inn right on the outskirts of town. I've got two beds if you want to crash."

I nodded. "That would be good. I need a release."

Robert glanced over at the door. "Looks like the convoy for the burial site is getting ready. I'll see you tonight."

I waved at my other cousin Liam as he headed for the door. Most of the people were strangers to me, and I tried to decide whether I should start drinking now or wait until the evening.

Maybe it was time to make a change and fight my impulses.

A voice said, "Are you Joseph Riley?"

I faced a man about six feet tall with a lean build, neatly trimmed salt and pepper hair, and a meticulously groomed beard. He wore a suit that looked like it cost more than my last book advance.

"Not if you have a subpoena," I said. I meant it as a joke, but with the way my day was going, it could have happened.

The man made a facial expression that suggested a smile but was far too practiced and fake. "I'm Benjamin Clarke, with Bayson and Clarke."

He didn't offer a hand to shake, and neither did I.

"I'm representing Richard Riley's estate," he said in a clipped tone. "I take it you received our notice about the probate and release of the will?"

I tried to appear wise. "I've been in the middle of a divorce, so my mail might not get to me," I explained. That wasn't the truth. I hadn't been looking at my damn mail. I'd been on a bender that had started about a week before. "What does that have to do with me?"

"There is a bequest for you in the will," he said, handing me a business card with a local address.

I stared at the card in my hand. "A bequest to me?" I repeated.

He seemed nonplussed by my response. "Yes. We are meeting after the burial, as we need all the heirs to sign releases. Could you be at my office at 5 PM today?"

"Sure," I said, and glanced at my watch. It was two-thirty, and where did I have to go?

"I'll see you then," he said with that rigid smile, and followed the group out to their cars.

I stood staring at the card in my hand, my mind racing.

What could Uncle Rick have left me?

TO BE CONTINUED
IN

Ghost
Writer

A Supernatural Suspense Mystery

Also by Arjay Lewis

Doctor Wise Series
Fire In The Mind
Seduction In The Mind
Reunion In The Mind
Haunted In The Mind
Devotion In The Mind
Asylum In The Mind
Specter In The Mind
Vengeance In The Mind
Echoes In The Mind
Infection In The Mind
Justice In The Mind
Ritual In The Mind
Vanished In The Mind

Horror
The Muse
Kept In The Dark
The Vanishing
Digger
Ghost Writer

Romantic Suspense
(with Debra Snow)
A Study In Murder

NYPD Wizard Detective
The Wizards Of Central Park West
The Vampires Of Greenwich Village
The Werewolves Of Washington Square

About The Author

Known as the "Wizard Of Odd." Arjay Lewis is an actor, magician, and multi-award-winning author.

I write tales of the strange and the horrifying.

I have spent my life as an entertainer, amusing people as a street-performer in the 1970s; a Broadway and casino artist in the 1980s; a party performer in the 1990s and 2000s; a cruise ship performer in the 2010s.

Stories have always been in my mind, and I have been writing since the 1990s. My reason to write is simple: to entertain. I write the type of books that I like to read: murder mysteries, strange tales of unnatural gifts, odd happenings and horror.

Please visit my web site and sign up for my mailing list to be "in the know" for upcoming books. Visit me on Facebook, Twitter, or my Amazon Author page.

And thank you for reading. You are the reason I write.

www.arjaylewis.com
www.facebook.com/arjaylewis
www.twitter.com/arjaylewiswrite
www.amazon.com/Arjay-Lewis

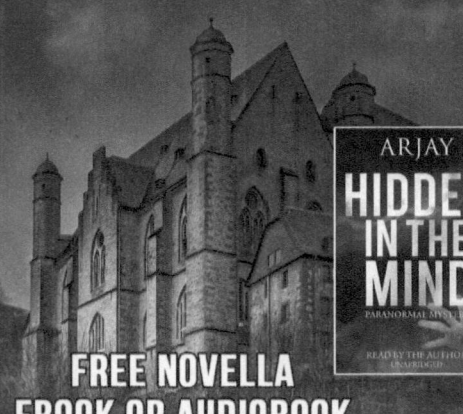